HER LOST SOUL

HELEN PHIFER

Storm
PUBLISHING

This is a work of fiction. Names, characters, business, events and incidents are the products of the author's imagination. Any resemblance to actual persons, living or dead, or actual events is purely coincidental.

Ebook ISBN: 978-1-80508-518-8
Paperback ISBN: 978-1-80508-519-5

Cover design: Blacksheep
Cover images: Shutterstock

Published by Storm Publishing.
For further information, visit:
www.stormpublishing.co

ALSO BY HELEN PHIFER

Detective Maria Miller

The Haunting on West 10th Street

Her Lost Soul

Annie Graham Series

The Ghost House

The Secrets of the Shadows

The Forgotten Cottage

The Lake House

The Girls in the Woods

The Face Behind the Mask

The Good Sisters

Lake View House

Detective Lucy Harwin Series

Dark House

Dying Breath

Last Light

Beth Adams Series

The Girl in the Grave

The Girls in the Lake

Detective Morgan Brookes

One Left Alive

The Killer's Girl

The Hiding Place

First Girl to Die

Find the Girl

Sleeping Dolls

Silent Angel

Their Burning Graves

Hold Your Breath

Stolen Darlings

PROLOGUE

BEACON HILL ASYLUM

December 12th, 2023

They left the warmth and safety of the car to go out into the darkness. Ryan had parked a few blocks away, so their arrival wouldn't stand out and give the security guards reason to check them out. Riley peered upwards at the old building. The frost-coated turrets and boarded windows could be seen peeking through the overgrown tangle of trees and shrubs, bare of their greenery that winter brought, giving the grounds that skirted the edges of the place an eerie feeling of desolation. The four of them—Drew, Noah, Riley and Ryan—had been laughing loudly and fooling around until they'd driven through the gates for the abandoned hospital. Now, they were silent.

Dressed entirely in black, they looked a formidable sight. If their age didn't give them away, they could have been mistaken for a SWAT team, minus the guns. Drew lingered by the car and Riley knew without asking that she'd changed her mind. Her friend had never been a hundred percent into this idea in the first place and Riley felt bad that she'd begged her to come along. Earlier that evening they'd stuffed their backpacks with cameras, flashlights, EMF meters, digital recorders, drinks and whatever else they thought they might need for a night spent investigating the old hospital. They knew they couldn't put off paying it a visit any longer. Later that week, the contractors would begin ripping the place to shreds.

The new owners were strict; the hospital was out of bounds to everyone. Guards patrolled around the clock and had erected heavy steel gates that were always chained up at the front. Ryan led the way. He'd been inside the grounds before and knew a way they could get in without being caught. The rest of the property was surrounded by a crumbling red brick wall, but Ryan knew where it was low enough to clamber over if you were tall or if someone gave you a leg up.

Riley hovered behind, while Noah and Drew silently pressed themselves through the overgrown mess of trees to get to the perimeter. A dog barked somewhere in the distance.

Ryan whispered, "It's okay, there are no guard dogs on the premises. I checked a couple of days ago. I climbed over and wandered around. None came running."

Drew shook her head. "Praise the Lord. I don't want to get my ass savaged by an angry dog before we even get close."

Riley grinned. Drew was funny, even if she was a bit of a scaredy cat when it came to stuff like this. It was a surprise that she'd come at all, after their last attempt at exploring the hospital. She'd insisted on sitting in Ryan's car while they'd all wandered around the perimeter in the dark before calling it a night.

Ryan made the climb over the wall look easy. He waited on the other side to give Drew a hand down. Next came Riley, then Noah. When all four of them were safely on the ground, they turned to look at the building, which was steeped in darkness. Its turrets and dramatic Gothic details would have made it the perfect place to film *The Munsters*. Riley was in love. There was something about lonely and unloved old buildings like this that made her want to explore them even more.

"She's beautiful. Come on, let's go before we get caught. I have to see what she looks like from the inside before she's torn to pieces."

Drew muttered, "Beautiful in a Frankenstein's monster way, Riley. It's creepy as hell."

Again, Ryan led the way. They didn't approach the front entrance—that was too obvious, and they didn't know if there were cameras installed above it. Instead, Ryan took them around the back.

Drew whispered, "So many windows, so many boards. Have you got a screwdriver?"

Ryan nodded. "I loosened one the other day on my recon. We only have to unscrew them a little."

He led them to a small window; it was too small for Riley's liking.

"Could you not have picked one of the bigger ones, Ryan? My ass might get stuck."

He smiled. "No one will notice if this is missing. If we removed one of the huge ones it will stand out too much."

He had a point. Noah passed him a screwdriver and Riley shared a glance with Drew.

"How amazing is this? Are you excited?"

"Excited? I'm scared, Riley, aren't you?"

She shrugged. "A little, but I can't wait to explore."

Drew gave her a look that questioned her sanity, but Riley ignored it.

Next moment the board was on the ground and Ryan, who was tall and skinny, climbed through the window. Riley followed him, and Noah followed behind her. All three of them waited for Drew's face to appear. When it didn't, Riley pulled herself up onto the small windowsill and peered down at her friend.

"Are you coming? We have to hurry. You'll get caught hanging around out there, and besides, if you wait outside it will be just you and the ghosts from the cemetery."

Drew paused. She looked around the overgrown garden at the gnarled trees and shadows.

"I don't know if we should be doing this."

"Why? We're not hurting anyone. We're just taking a look at it before they come and tear it to shreds. If anything, we're doing them a favor by documenting it one last time." Riley wasn't sure who *they* were, but it was true they weren't there to damage or steal anything. They just wanted to film it, snap some photos and maybe see if they could see a ghost or two.

The dog that had been barking earlier began to howl as the almost full moon broke through the inky clouds in the sky, illuminating the unloved, forlorn gardens as if someone had turned on a spotlight and aimed it directly at them.

Riley hissed, "Come on, Drew."

Drew took one last look around, then clambered onto the window ledge and through the window.

Noah and Ryan both clapped, and Drew gave them the finger. Riley smiled. She loved her friendship group. They'd been friends ever since they were little kids. They were as geeky and weird as she was, and she wouldn't have it any other way. All of them lost any popularity contests at school. Riley, with her beachy, blonde waves and blue eyes, looked like she would fit in with the cheerleaders and jocks, but because of who her dad was the rest of their classmates scorned her. Nobody wanted her to tell tales on them after football games when the students would party hard to celebrate or commiserate their performance. Not that she was the tale-telling type. Ryan and Noah, meanwhile, were members of the science club and spent hours building radio systems and other stuff Riley didn't understand. She was more interested in computer programming than science, but each to their own. All of them shared one common interest, however: their love of ghost stories, and so it had made perfect sense when they had decided to form their own paranormal club.

With flashlights out, they entered a small room that must have once been a closet. Papers were scattered all over the floor and the air was filled with the earthy smell of damp and decay. Next, Ryan led them down the hallway and through a doorway, into a room so big it could have fit all their high school class in and still had room to maneuver.

"This must have been some party house," muttered Noah.

Riley smirked. Noah didn't like to party, but he was right; it would have made a great frat house.

Drew shook her head. "I don't like it... I don't think we should be in here. It feels wrong."

"We're just having a look around," said Riley, "documenting it for the history books kind of thing."

There was a shuffling noise as something heavy crossed the ceiling above, making them all stop.

Drew whispered, "What the hell is that?"

"Racoons, mice, possums maybe," replied Ryan.

They waited. Riley didn't say anything, but she was sure it had been the sound of feet—human feet. It didn't happen again, so they carried on.

"There's supposed to be a music room with one of those huge church organs inside that apparently plays on its own. Imagine if we caught that on camera?" said Ryan. "There's also a few of those treatment rooms where they gave the patients electric shock therapy and God knows what else. I want to see inside those, get them all photographed."

Ryan was the most excited to be here. He was the one with a lifelong fascination with TV ghost shows and had the greatest passion for empty, abandoned buildings. He'd been Riley's best friend ever since kindergarten, and she'd follow him anyplace he went because he'd always been there for her, even throughout the tragedies of the last few years, and she would always be there for him.

He pushed open the peeling, warped door to a room that had been the rec room. It was grand enough to have been a ballroom, with a rotting, wooden parquet floor. Huge columns were intricately carved with cherubs that must have once been painted white and were now daubed with terrible graffiti. The columns held up a series of arches and the walls behind them were shelved from floor to ceiling with only a couple of tattered, damp books lying discarded. Riley walked straight over to them; books were her one true love and she wanted to see what kind were deemed "recommended reading" for a hospital full of psychiatric patients. Her three friends were already filing out of the door, but she would catch them up.

Picking up a mottled, green leather cover she was surprised to read part of the word *Frankenstein* in faded gold letters. This and *Dracula* were Riley's favorite stories. The book was in much better condition than the one next to it which was unreadable. It was swollen, bloated like a rotting corpse. This thought made her flinch. Where had it come from? She'd never in her life described anything as being like a rotting corpse.

That moment a noise above made her head jolt backwards. This time it was clearly footsteps. They were light and hurried, as if someone was rushing around trying to get things done. Riley figured the book didn't belong to anyone now except for maybe the ghosts, so pushed it into her backpack, deciding she would add it to her collection. As she did so, a cold breeze enveloped her neck and shoulders. Icy fingers felt as if they were touching her skin. She opened her mouth to scream when she heard a loud cry from somewhere down the hall. Snapping herself out of her trance, Riley ran to see who had screamed. It had sounded like Ryan.

"Where are you guys?" she called. "Who's screaming?"

The corridor was empty. The scream had come from

further down the hallway. She didn't feel as brave on her own. The beams from the ceiling light wavered around, up and down. Riley heard her friends talking in a room upstairs, and she realized that it must have been their footsteps crossing the floor above her. Ryan had probably jumped out on Drew and scared the crap out of her. This made her sigh with relief. She was doing a better job of scaring herself than Noah or Ryan could ever do.

"Come on, you guys, you're not even funny, and why didn't you wait for me?"

Riley burst into the room she'd heard the voices coming from, shining the flashlight around. Seeing what was inside, an icy cold liquid filled her veins, so much so that she couldn't speak. This was the entrance to a ward. There were two long rows of rusted metal bedframes and discarded, overturned chairs. As far as she could see it was completely empty. Although the beam of her flashlight didn't reach the dark corners at the end of the room, she knew her friends wouldn't be so cruel as to hide there in the pitch black.

The faint smell of wood smoke filled the air. Then she saw the glowing embers of a small fire that had been lit in an old metal drawer, a little way inside the room. Someone must have lit it trying to keep warm, she realized. Riley felt bad. If this was the best place someone had to call home, that was so sad. Then the thought passed through her mind that whoever was living here could be nearby—and they might be dangerous. She shivered.

Turning to go back into the corridor, she saw with a jolt of fear that someone was standing there, blocking her exit. Through the cracked panes of glass in the door she could see they had straggly, long black hair. Their face was hidden because they were leaning forwards, staring down at the floor. Finding it hard to breathe, she cupped a hand over her mouth to stop herself from screaming. Who was this person? It couldn't be Drew, who had chestnut hair tied back in a neat ponytail, and both Ryan and Noah had short, brown hair. The figure on the other side wasn't moving. It was just waiting there. Was this the person living in this awful room? Did they know she was there?

Pulling out her phone, she hit Ryan's number. To her alarm, there was no signal. Now she really started to panic. Whoever was on the other side of the door didn't seem to notice her presence because their head was still bent. Riley stepped back into the shadows, in case they suddenly looked up and made eye contact with her. She had a terrible, foreboding sense that if she looked at their face, she'd be snared like an animal caught in a trap. Her legs and hands trembled as she pressed the off button on the flashlight. Silently, she prayed the person on the other side of the door hadn't seen her.

"Riley, Riley." She heard Ryan and Drew calling her name. The blackness in front of her was so consuming that she couldn't see her hand in front of her face. She wanted to call out to them, to warn them about the person blocking her exit from the ward. She turned the flashlight back on and shone it in the direction of the door. Whoever had been there was gone. The relief rushed from her, propelling her forwards. She ran for the door, threw it open, and crashed straight into Noah. They both screamed, as did Drew.

Ryan laughed. "Oh my God, you got us good," he said. "That scared me—why were you hiding in there on your own, you weirdo?"

"I thought you were inside. I heard voices but when I went in, it was empty. Then I turned around and there was a person standing on the other side. Did you see them?"

Noah shook his head. "We haven't seen anyone; we've been all over this place looking for you."

"They had long, straggly hair," Riley went on. "I couldn't see their face."

"Must have been some homeless dude. Maybe they stay here."

What Ryan suggested made sense. In any case, it was easier to accept than what she had been thinking. "I don't know, maybe. Whoever it was, they had a fire burning in the old ward that was almost out. Hey, don't leave me alone again. In fact, I think we should leave. That person might be dangerous."

Drew shook her head. "Are you kidding? This place is amazing. I want to go up in the tower—apparently some famous actor's mother killed herself up there back in the day. There's four of us. Even if it's a drunken homeless person they won't want to bother us, not when we have two big guys to protect us."

Riley shrugged. "Okay." Deep down inside her stomach she knew that it wasn't okay. It wasn't okay at all. They shouldn't be here, and whoever she'd seen didn't think so either. Why had Drew had this sudden change of heart, when she'd been so scared before? Now she was practically buzzing with excitement. Riley didn't understand it. All she wanted to do was go home.

They walked in a line down the hallway. The air was much cooler now. Ryan held the EMF meter which kept going crazy, and Noah had the digital recorder. As they made their way in and out of rooms, Riley felt exhausted, as if she was carrying a heavy load on her back. Her stomach churned like she was walking on a boat and didn't have her sea legs. Her instincts were screaming at her to get out of this place, but fear and a sense of loyalty kept her with her friends. She was petrified of seeing the dark-haired figure again and so she had no choice but to follow them.

The rooms further down the corridor were much plusher than those they'd been inside before. They must have been for the wealthier patients; they were more like hotel rooms. Although there was no furniture left, the walls were decorated in soothing pastel, floral colors. The carpets, which had decayed into sodden, spongy clumps, must have been good quality to have survived this long.

Finally finding her voice, Riley spoke. "Marilyn Monroe stayed here."

Ryan turned to look at her. "She did, in this room?"

"I don't know what room, you idiot, but I read that she stayed here for a while before the end of her marriage and the whole Kennedy thing blew up."

"Imagine being here because you're unwell. You go to the bathroom and see Marilyn Monroe coming out of her room." Ryan shook his head. "You'd think you had either died and gone to heaven or completely lost it."

Riley always felt sad whenever she thought about the lonely life that Marilyn had led. She would've been a good friend to her, would've looked out for her, if she'd been around back then. She peered through the cracked window down onto the overgrown gardens.

"Whatever room she was in, Marilyn would have looked down on this view. I bet it was much nicer when she was here. Isn't there supposed to be a pool house? Do you think they left her alone or do you think they'd have kept bothering her for autographs? It's so sad what happened. It makes my heart ache just thinking about her being so lonely."

"It was a hospital," replied Drew. "I hope they left her alone and helped her find some peace whilst she was here."

A loud metallic clatter from above made Drew and Noah shriek. Ryan jumped, and, silent with terror, Riley felt her heart race so hard it threatened to explode from her chest. This place scared her beyond belief, and she was sure that if she screamed, whoever she'd seen earlier would come back for her.

Ryan whispered, "What was that?"

"Time to leave is what that was," replied Riley, her voice so low it was barely audible.

They stood huddled together, waiting for something else to happen. It didn't.

"This is an old wreck—things are going to be falling to pieces! It's why they're knocking it down. Look at you lot, screaming like a bunch of losers." Ryan laughed. "Come on, you pussies, let's go take a look at the tower, get some photos and make our way out."

A voice whispered so softly in Riley's ear that she couldn't be sure that she'd heard it. "Don't go in the tower." It was gentle, like a cool breeze against the soft skin of her neck.

Turning around, there was no one there; whoever had given her that warning had gone or had never been there in the first place. For a split second she wondered if she was having some kind of episode, a mental breakdown. Was being inside this old asylum affecting her more than she could have ever imagined? Or were there actually ghosts here?

They carried on walking, all of them a little edgy after the loud noise. Investigating a room at the far end of the corridor, they saw a huge chair, its leather worn away so much that there was a fern growing out of the damp material. It resembled a dental chair, only it had worn leather straps, one either side of it.

"Oh Lord, I thought they'd have taken away all of this stuff," whispered Riley.

In the corner was an overturned, rusted wheelchair. Riley poked Ryan with her finger. "Do you think that's what fell over and made that clatter against the broken tiles on the floor?"

He was busy snapping photos. "Could be—how did it fall though?"

Riley didn't want to think about the how.

Noah pushed Drew forwards. "Go get in the treatment chair, Drew, so we can take a photo, pretend you've been lobotomized."

Drew giggled. Showing off, she flicked her long hair over

her shoulder, gave Noah her best seductive look and clambered onto the chair. "Ooh," she wailed, "this is damp and feels weird."

"Get off there," hissed Riley, who had a bad feeling inside her stomach.

Instead, Drew lay down and spread out her arms, rolling her eyes to the back of her head pretending to be getting electric shocks, her body jerking. Noah laughed, and Ryan joined in.

Riley, who was horrified, shouted, "Get the fuck off it, Drew. Have some respect."

A crack filled the air and a large chunk of plaster plummeted down from the ceiling, catching the side of Drew's head. She let out a high-pitched screech as the masonry sliced open her temple. Scrambling to get off the chair, she slipped on the damp leather and fell forwards, landing on the floor with a loud thud.

"Ouch," she cried, "I'm bleeding."

Noah helped her up, a look of panic on his face. He shone his flashlight at the cut on her head.

"It's just a scratch. It's more bruised than anything. Are you okay?"

"No, I'm not okay. I was almost killed."

Riley shook her head; Drew wasn't a drama major for nothing. "You're fine, it's just bleeding a little." She pulled a scrunchie from her jeans pocket. It was the only thing she had that she could use to dab the blood.

"Thanks, but what if I get some disease?"

Riley shook her head. "We're not in the Amazon rainforest, I'm sure you'll be fine. You shouldn't have been messing around like that. It's disrespectful to the patients who lived and died here. We don't know what kind of horrible torture they went through strapped on that chair."

"People died here?" Drew replied. "I thought this was one

of those rich places like the ones where famous people go for rehab."

"Yes, people died here. Before it was a private hospital it was a state lunatic asylum for the criminally insane. There were lots of deaths—natural, suicide and murder."

"Murder?"

As the words left Drew's mouth they seemed to freeze in the air, and Riley realized the room had turned icy cold, so her breath was a visible fog. They were no longer alone.

Feeling an impending sense of doom, Riley shouted, "Run!"

Ryan didn't need telling twice. "She's right. We have to go, someone... or something is coming."

A low growl pierced the air. Drew ran out first, then Noah with Ryan close behind. Riley was frozen to the spot. Her legs shook, and she couldn't think of a time that she'd ever been this scared. The others had run off and left her behind. Once again, she was alone.

* * *

It was like a cartoon chase. Drew led the way and Noah followed close behind her. Ryan came thundering down the stairs, almost slamming into them both as he reached the bottom.

"Where's Riley?" Drew whispered, breathing heavily.

"Behind me." Ryan turned around, but Riley was not behind him. "Oh, crap, she was like a nanosecond ago."

All three of them stared at each other, eyes wide, out of breath, hearts beating wildly.

"Who—or what—was that?" Ryan asked.

"I don't know," replied Drew. "Did you see them?"

He nodded. "I thought I saw someone. It terrified me."

Noah stood at the bottom of the stairs, one hand gripping

the rail. "Riley?" It wasn't a shout, more of a subtle whisper. There was no answer. "Riley?" he tried again, louder this time.

Ryan grabbed his arm, lifting a finger to his lips. From somewhere above came a muffled dragging, shuffling sound.

"Oh God, we can't leave her up there." Drew was trembling. She took out her phone. "We need to call the cops—what if it's that weird person she saw? They might be dangerous."

"We'll get in trouble; we can't call them," insisted Ryan. "And isn't her dad working tonight? He'll go batshit with us if he finds out we've been sneaking around in here. We'll all get arrested."

"You go look for her then," said Drew. "You left her behind."

Ryan shook his head. "No, I didn't, she was right behind me."

Noah looked at the pair of them. "Come on, we'll all go back and look for her. She's probably hiding."

"What about that person?" asked Ryan. "They might be waiting up there for the rest of us."

"We can't leave her here, dude," replied Noah. "We're going to have to go back and find her. Or call the cops. You choose. Riley's dad or the homeless dude?"

None of them wanted to face Riley's dad. He was six foot eight of pure muscle and a stickler for the law. He would probably arrest them all, even Riley, for trespassing, not to mention lecture them for hours about sneaking in here. Drew nodded. "Let's go find her."

She took the first step up, saying a jumbled prayer to Saint Michael for protection. She'd seen ghost hunters on TV shows say prayers like that. Ryan and Noah followed behind. Some heroes they were, cowering behind her like a pair of pussies.

"Riley!" she called out. Ryan grabbed her arm, shushing her.

"Drew, *shut it* or they'll know we're here, whoever *they* are.

We've gotta find her. We can't sneak around hoping she'll come out of hiding. She won't know whether it's us or that thing. Besides, there's safety in numbers. Noah, make sure you're recording this on your phone, okay? Just in case." A violent shudder wracked her entire body.

Ryan whispered, "Are you okay?"

Drew nodded, not trusting herself to speak. She wasn't okay at all; she was terrified beyond any fear she'd known her entire life. Someone was up here shuffling around. Where were they? Had they got Riley?

The upstairs was huge, and she knew they'd be better splitting up, but she was far too afraid to walk around on her own. She pointed to the room they'd run from, crossed her fingers, praying to God that nothing was in there except Riley, who was rooted to the spot too scared to move. As if in slow motion, they trudged toward the room. A putrid stench lingered in the air like when the garbage men had gone on strike that summer and everyone's garbage had been left on the front sidewalk baking in the sun.

"What is that smell?" Noah whispered.

"The smell of the undead." Drew's voice was barely audible. She'd no idea where her words had come from.

"What?" asked Ryan.

She didn't repeat what she'd said because she was scaring herself. They were almost there; the room was a few steps away.

"Riley," she called, "you can come out."

They were greeted by a silence so heavy Drew could feel the weight of it on her shoulders, pressing down. Her fingers clenched the flashlight tightly as she stepped through the doorway. Shining the flashlight around the room, she saw that it was empty. No Riley, no one hiding in the shadows. The overturned wheelchair was still on its side, but one wheel spun around as if someone or something was pushing it. Drew looked at Ryan, they all looked at the chair, then they ran from the room.

Drew heard a noise behind her. She stopped to check whether it was Riley, while the guys continued down the stairs, back to where they'd first entered the building what seemed like hours ago. With no sign of her friend, Drew followed the boys down the stairs. She didn't call out. They were making enough noise between them that Riley should have heard and come to join them. Noah pushed himself through the window first, then Drew, and Ryan threw himself out last.

"Where the hell is Riley?" Drew asked, panting, as they gathered in the night air.

Noah stared back into the blackness they'd just escaped from. "Oh God, we have to call the cops because I'm not going back in there. I just can't, man, I'm shaking too much."

Ryan took out his phone and dialed 911. "I don't know who we should be more scared of. Riley's dad, or whoever was inside that building."

Deep down, he knew the answer.

ONE

NEW YORK, PRESENT DAY

Homicide Detective Maria Miller stared down at the street below. People were going about their business in typical New York fashion. Heads down, ear buds in, talking loudly in one-way conversations.

Living near the New York University in Greenwich Village ensured there was always something happening. The area was lively and although her apartment block was rundown on the outside, inside it was a different matter. Maria took great pride in her open-spaced, whitewashed walls. She had no kids to mark them with sticky fingerprints. No pets, either, because they weren't allowed, and she didn't have the time to care for anyone else. Occasionally she let Harrison Williams take her out on dates, but they weren't serious, or she wasn't serious anyway. He was a good guy, and super-rich. Even though he could have any woman he wanted, he never gave up on Maria, which was sweet, she guessed. But she was happy with how their relationship was going. In other words, slowly. Living her life on her terms made everything less complicated.

A horn blared from below and she realized she'd lost track of time. Frankie Conroy, her police partner who was also her best friend, was now probably having a fit that she wasn't waiting on the sidewalk. Grabbing her purse, she threw it over her shoulder and rushed out of the door, stopping to make sure it was secure before heading to the stairs. She'd let a killer inside once; it wouldn't happen again.

"Would you look at who the cat dragged in? What took you so long, kid?"

She sat next to Frankie and glared. "Don't call me kid. It's insulting."

"Yeah? You find that offensive because you know I could call you a hell of a lot worse."

"Yikes. Someone did not feed you today, Conroy. You're such a grouch when you're hungry."

"I am not."

She ignored him. He pulled away from the sidewalk. "Well, now that you mention it, I could do with some breakfast."

"It's almost noon and you haven't had breakfast?" Maria frowned. "You need to take care of yourself better, Frankie. What if your blood sugar gets low and you pass out when you're driving?"

He rolled his eyes. "So dramatic."

"Okay, then. If that's too dramatic, let's stick with *you're a miserable son of a bitch when you're hungry*."

"Better," Frankie replied. "Have you got anything in that bag of yours I can eat?" He looked over at her hopefully.

Maria shook her head. "Where are we going? You can run in to Sam's Deli on the way and grab something."

"Beacon."

She blinked hard. "What?"

"Beacon."

"I heard you the first time. Why the hell are we driving ninety minutes to go to Beacon?"

He pointed to the back seat where a brown folder lay, with a page of a crime report peeking out. Leaning back, she grabbed and opened it. She scanned the document, and realized it was a missing person's report.

"What, so Beacon have no officers to deal with a missing person?"

"They have plenty. Look at the address of where she's missing from."

"Beacon Hill. I've never heard of it."

"You've never heard of Beacon Hill, seriously?"

"No, I haven't." She flushed with annoyance. He really could be a pain in the ass when he wanted to be.

"Where have you been?"

"Frankie, compared to me you're ancient. I think you forget that."

"Ten years older is not ancient."

She laughed. "It is to me. Tell me what Beacon Hill is and put me out of my misery."

"It's an old hospital. It's been shut down for over thirty years now. Abandoned and from the photographs I saw online it's as creepy as hell. Looks like one of those places that crazy *Ghost Adventures* crew go visit."

She knew *Ghost Adventures*. She used to watch the TV show until she got sucked into the living nightmare that was West 10th Street a couple of months ago. Now, she slept with a night light on, always triple-checked that her front door was locked, and never watched anything remotely scary. Unlike Frankie, who had binge-watched every single episode of the show in the name of research.

Maria eyed him skeptically. "I still don't understand why we're going all the way out to Beacon."

"Give me a second, I'm about to tell you." He parked the car outside Sam's Deli on Waverley Place. "But first, run in and get me a bagel, coffees, too. Whatever you want, I'm buying." He pushed two twenties into her hand.

With a deep sigh, Maria got out of the car. She ran up the

steps into the deli where, as usual, life was incredibly normal. People were eating early lunches or late breakfasts on their way to and from work. She envied them. The patrons of Sam's Deli didn't have trouble sleeping at night for fear of something dark and evil coming to get them. After what had happened, Maria had thought that she'd be okay in time. She'd been so sure that she wasn't horribly affected by what had happened that she'd agreed to run the new department with Frankie, to deal with exactly those kinds of unexplainable incidents, after being swayed by the generous pay increase as a sweetener. But she hadn't really understood back then just how much the events on West 10th Street would affect her life outside of work.

Placing her order at the counter, she sat on one of the high stools.

"Penny for them, Maria." She recognized Sam's deep, throaty voice, the result of smoking way too many Marlboros.

"Morning, Sam. Oh, you know, just the usual. Work, dead people, that kind of stuff."

He shook his head. "You're too fine a lady to be dealing with a job like that. Come work with me and the worst stress you'll have is getting someone's order wrong."

She laughed. "Tempting, Sam, but I'd miss the excitement. I love it really."

He shrugged with a glint in his eye. "I can be exciting." Next moment, he was yelling, "Ouch, Marge, you're too rough."

Marge had appeared next to him. Her arms were folded across her chest, a notebook sat in her apron pocket and a pencil was tucked behind her ear. Sam rubbed the ear that she'd just tugged down on, hard.

"Is he giving you a hard time, honey?" Marge asked. "He's too old and it's too early to be so vulgar."

Maria grinned. "He's not. In fact, he offered me a job."

The eye roll Marge gave was of an epic proportion. "Jeez. Well, I bet you're so tempted you're gonna go straight down to the precinct and hand in your resignation. C'mon, Sam, Maria and Frankie are two of the good guys. They're a team you can't split up. Together they make the Village a much safer place to be. And you want her to come here and serve coffee all day, just so you can ogle her?"

Sam shook his head, the picture of innocence. "Just trying to help a girl out and give her options." He passed over two huge bagels wrapped tightly in aluminum foil.

The young girl at the coffee machine, who only looked like a kid, pressed lids down on two cappuccinos and passed them across the counter. Maria smiled at her, and the girl almost smiled back. She was new, or at least fairly new. Maria hadn't seen her before, but she reminded her of someone she knew with her tattooed arms, purple spiky hair and Grateful Dead T-shirt, only she wasn't sure who.

"Thanks," Maria said. "Catch you later." She threw a twenty on the counter, even though Sam always told them their food was on the house. He was a good guy, and Marge was a sweetheart, despite her tough exterior doing a pretty good job of convincing you otherwise. They would make a great couple. Maria wished they would realize that and get their act together, instead of wasting time.

Opening the car door she found Frankie with his head back, eyes wide open, lips apart, head lolled to one side, doing an amazing job of looking like he'd died in his seat. She ignored him and slammed the door shut.

"If you're dead, you won't want this bagel, will you?"

His head snapped up. "I could have starved to death you were in there so long."

"It's not too late to go to drama school, you know. There's plenty of roles for old guys who are always in a bad mood."

"Pass me my bagel. My gut hurts I'm so hungry."

She smiled and handed him one. As she leaned closer the faint smell of stale bourbon filled her nostrils.

"Why are you so hungry? Did you eat last night? And why didn't you make breakfast before you left this morning?"

"Of course I ate something, but I had a little night cap afterwards, and then got a call from an old friend in Beacon PD asking me if I'd take a look at this missing kid case."

"I worry about you, Frankie. You do know bourbon isn't going to solve your problems and bring Christie back?"

"Good, because I don't want her back. I just want to forget my marriage ever happened. Sometimes I need a little help to blot it all out, otherwise I can't sleep at night. At my age you need all the beauty sleep you can get."

He unwrapped his bagel and took a huge bite, letting out a sigh as a dribble of melted butter ran down his chin. "This is great," he said through a mouthful of mashed bagel, bacon and cheese. Maria let him eat, passing him a napkin, then picked up the report again.

"It's a seventeen-year-old girl who's missing?"

He nodded. "My old pal works with Riley's father. The girl was out with her friends, and then she was gone. Pft, just like that into thin air. They've had the dogs out, air searches combing the area, you name it. He asked if we could come take a look."

"And the lieutenant is fine with this?"

"Absolutely. Gave us his blessing and said it comes under our remit."

"What are you not telling me? Why *us*? How is this under our remit?"

"It's an old private mental facility with a tarnished track record and... shall we say, a fair few deaths to its name. Do you remember the College Kid Killer from years ago, back in the early aughts?"

"You mean it's a creepy old asylum? And no, the College Kid Killer doesn't ring any bells."

"It's meant to be haunted, or at least all the local school kids say it is. They break in regularly, daring each other to go ghost hunting, that kind of crap. Fifteen years ago, there was a string of missing college kids from a couple of towns over. All teenagers. I think there were four of them. They found the guy hiding out in the hospital. Only found three bodies, despite turning the place upside down. There's still one girl, Courtney Moon, missing after all these years."

"Do you think the case from fifteen years ago could be related to this new one? Is the perp still in prison? He must be."

"No idea." Frankie stuffed the rest of the bagel into his mouth then licked his fingers clean, took a sip of his coffee and started the car.

Meanwhile, Maria researched the address in the report on her phone. An uneasy feeling grew in her gut as she waited for the pictures to load. West 10th Street had looked like an everyday brownstone from the outside and yet inside it had been the scariest place on earth. Scrolling through the images, she thought that the old hospital looked like her worst nightmare come true. It was everything ghost hunters dreamed of, with its boarded-up windows, ivy-clad turrets and overgrown gardens. Knowing that it had been the hiding place for a serial killer made her blood run cold.

As they left the city center behind, Maria couldn't decide what was worse: the normal-looking brownstone that had been a hiding place for evil. Or the hospital of horrors they were about to face.

TWO

As Frankie drove into Beacon, Maria looked up from her phone. She'd been glued to it the whole journey, reading about the Beacon Hill Asylum and all its former lives, from starting out as a private home to becoming a hospital for the rich and famous. She read that Marilyn Monroe had been a patient for four days along with many other Hollywood stars, including Frances Farmer. It had been bought by a millionaire in the early 2000s. He'd intended to convert it back into a home but soon after moving in he died by throwing himself out of the turreted tower window on a stormy night during a power cut.

Reaching the golf course, Frankie took a right and turned onto Beacon House Lane. The narrow, tree-lined road bordered the edge of a forest. There was a huge fallen tree trunk to the side of the road before the turn off to the gated drive which led up to the old house. Maria took in the size of the black metal gates, the security fencing and signs that read *No Trespassing*. On the drive, she'd read pages of articles about Malcolm Collins, the College Kid Killer. She'd seen arrest pictures of him being led out of the hospital with his long, straggly black hair covering his eyes, and the uneven, gap-toothed grin he had on his face as he stared at the camera.

"Wow, those kids must have been either pretty brave or goddamn stupid to even go into these grounds."

"I've got a bad feeling about this one, Maria."

"Frankie, you always have a bad feeling about every single job. And if that's the case, why the hell did you drag me all this way?"

He nodded in agreement. She didn't tell him that she had a bad feeling, too. More than a bad feeling, it was a sense of foreboding that they were entering a place that should never be disturbed. The forlorn-looking Victorian mansion came fully into view, and she shuddered. The boards on the windows didn't stop the place from looking as if it was something from a nightmare.

There was a Beacon PD pickup parked out front with two officers sitting inside. Maria stared up at the turret, the only window that wasn't boarded up, likely because it was too high. It had to be the one the old owner had thrown himself from. This place had certainly seen some terrible things in its time. Frankie stopped the car beside the pickup and was out of the door before Maria could unbuckle her belt. She placed the file on the back seat and left her purse on the floor, glad she was wearing boots today. Getting out, she smiled at the two officers who chatted with Frankie like long lost buddies.

"This is my partner, Maria. She's a ballbuster but she's okay, aren't you, Maria?"

She looked at him with an expression of *did you really just say that out loud?* Ignoring him, she held out her hand to each man in turn.

"Mike Walker," said the tallest of the men, "and this is Arnie Jackson."

"Maria Miller. So, do you want to run me through what you have and where the case is up to?"

She was in no mood for small talk; she wanted to do this and get out of here before it got dark. There was no way on this earth she was trailing through an abandoned mental asylum once the sun went down, not for anyone, not even Frankie.

"The missing girl is called Riley Holt, the chief's only daughter. As you can imagine he's struggling to come to terms with it. Her and her three friends thought they'd turn into Ghostbusters for a few hours and broke into the building two nights ago. Something happened in one of the old treatment rooms upstairs, they got scared and ran. Only, by the time they made it outside, Riley was nowhere to be seen. They searched the building for her, calling out her name. Then they finally got scared enough to call us."

"I'm going to need to speak to them," Maria said.

"We'll give you their home addresses," replied Officer Jackson.

Maria didn't miss the look that Officer Jackson gave to Officer Walker. It was one of clear discomfort, probably at having two city cops stick their noses in on their case.

Frankie also watched the two men carefully. "Are you going to show us around inside, then?" he asked.

Both officers looked as if they'd rather wrestle a grizzly bear than go inside the building.

Jackson nodded. "Sure thing, you bet we are."

Frankie patted his shoulder. "Great, but first tell Maria why you called us out."

"This place." Jackson stopped and glanced uncertainly at Walker. "This place is weird; things happen here that shouldn't, if you know what I'm saying. And it has a bad history. They found that killer hiding out here. Who knows what he did with the kid they never found?"

Maria wanted to hear him say it out loud. "What kind of weird things happen?"

Jackson sighed. "Noises, footsteps. You get the feeling that you're being watched no matter where you go. But you can't find anyone else around, that kind of thing."

"You think it's haunted?"

Jackson looked uncomfortable. "I don't know. I guess it must be."

"Place like this, with so many bad memories, painful experiences... all that negative energy gets imprinted on the surroundings." Maria paused. "But what do you think all that has to do with the whereabouts of Riley Holt? Could she have used its reputation for being haunted as an excuse to run away so no one would look for her? Have you checked out any local registered sex offenders? That to me would be the first thing to look at. I'm assuming you've already considered this, since, according to the report I read, the teenagers mentioned seeing someone inside whilst they were exploring?"

Walker's horrified expression told Maria that no, they hadn't taken this into consideration at all.

She continued, "Show us around and talk us through it."

Inside their police car, the radio set burst into life and Walker ran to answer it. "This is Walker."

The answer blared out for them all to hear. "Walker, there's been a high-risk escape from the hospital, all officers to attend the area, locate the patient and take them back."

"On our way, Dorothy."

He turned to Jackson. "Looks like we've gotta go."

Maria didn't miss the look of relief that washed over Jackson's clammy face.

He took a handkerchief from his back pocket and blotted his forehead. "Can you guys take a look on your own?" he asked. "You can't miss the trail where the crime scene techs have been."

Frankie nodded. "Do you often have hospital breaks?"

Jackson shook his head. "Rarely. This is the first one I've known of in a long time." He tossed a set of keys to Frankie.

"These are for the front door and entrance gates. Make sure to lock them. We used to have a tree trunk blocking the road to the gates but had to get it towed for all the vehicles to get access. Those young punks will stop at nothing to get inside and it's still a crime scene."

"Haven't you got a patrol guarding it?"

Officer Jackson scoffed. "There's not enough of us. The current owners hired a security firm and they do drive-bys and walk-throughs. But with it being a crime scene they're not around."

Both men jumped into the pickup. Walker revved the engine and turned it around so fast that gravel sprayed from under the tires, hitting Maria on the arm. They watched as the truck disappeared.

"Something tells me they'd rather chase an escaped patient than walk us through that building."

"You think so?"

"I know so. Have we got flashlights?"

"Unfortunately, we do."

She sighed. "Go get them. And Frankie..."

"What?"

She stared at him. "What the hell have you got us into? Do you really believe that this place is haunted?"

He shrugged, which she knew meant *yes, but I won't say it out loud in case anyone is listening.*

"God damn it."

Frankie grabbed two large flashlights from the trunk and passed one to her.

"How long do you think we have before it gets dark?"

"A couple of hours, at most."

She strode to the hospital's open front door, which sat underneath a red brick porch, furious that they'd been left unaccompanied to search this huge place without even knowing its layout. If she pretended that she didn't believe in ghosts, then she wouldn't see or hear any—or so she hoped. In any case, they were here to check out the location where a missing girl had last been seen. Those officers should have been concentrating on the possibility that somebody human was involved in this, not worrying about smoke and shadows.

Maria glanced up at the turreted tower and felt a shiver run the full length of her spine. A dark shape had appeared briefly in the grimy window. Someone was up there staring down at her. But that was impossible. The hospital was meant to be empty—unless it was Riley.

"We need to check out the tower."

"What is it?" Frankie asked warily.

"I think I saw someone up there watching us. It might be the girl. Maybe she's been hiding out here for some reason, avoiding the cops."

"Then she's avoided the search dogs, the search team, her friends, her pops, all to stay in this hellhole on her own. If she has, she needs a bed in a mental facility for sure, because no sane person would want to hide out in here."

Maria didn't say what was on her mind. That she had a strong feeling, deep down inside her gut, that it wasn't Riley Holt who had been watching her. But to know that for sure, she needed to rule it out. Stepping inside the Beacon Hill Asylum, her stomach churned until Sam's bagel threatened to come back up, along with her cappuccino.

She took a deep breath. *Here we go, again.*

THREE

The inside of the building smelled like rotten leaves and mold. The air was stale, despite the fact that the doors had been wide open for the last forty-eight hours while search teams and CSI combed the place.

"Christ, it stinks." Frankie looked just as queasy as she was. "Still think the kid is hiding out in here?"

Maria shrugged. "She may have found somewhere that doesn't smell like the whole building is decomposing."

He gave her a look as if she'd lost it. "I doubt that. The scent is seeping from the walls."

Maria glanced down at the floor, which was littered with broken glass, leaves and God knows what other detritus. It was damp, too, as well as almost pitch black. The entrance must have once been a grand reception area, with cut glass chandeliers that had since been broken and smashed and were probably what was crunching under their feet. In its prime, the semicircle desk wouldn't have looked out of place in a fancy hotel. Now the whole place gave off the scariest, saddest vibes Maria had ever felt. There was graffiti daubed on the walls, though she was relieved to see no symbols that might be connected to devil worship. She'd had her fill of that to last a lifetime.

Frankie's light shone upwards at the stairs that went up a couple of floors. He wasn't paying attention to the ground in front of him when he stepped in a huge puddle of dank old rainwater.

He screeched and jumped backwards. "Holy shit!"

Maria had to hide the smirk on her face. "Yeah, you better watch the puddles."

He glared at her, while trying to shake the water from his Italian leather brogues. "You could have warned me."

"I was looking around just like you."

"Jeez, my socks are all soggy. I hate soggy socks."

"Take them off."

"And walk around this place with bare feet? No, thank you."

"Then quit complaining and keep your eyes on the ground. Next time it could be a wide-ass hole in the floor you're stepping into, straight down into the cellars."

She made sure she walked around the stagnant water, not wanting to make the same mistake. They saw yellow markers left by the CSI at the bottom of the stairs.

"What are we doing?" asked Frankie. "Searching the whole building, or do we follow the yellow brick road to the top?"

"I'm not wasting hours in here, especially not when it's dark. There's no point. We'll follow the markers and go upstairs to where Riley was last seen. Try to find the way to the tower. And then we're out of here before it gets late."

"Sounds like a decent plan to me, boss."

She smiled but shook her head. "Asshole."

As they climbed the stairs there was the muffled sound of hurried footsteps above them, as if a person was rushing or running somewhere.

Maria turned back to Frankie and whispered, "See, I told you someone was in here."

He nodded. "Do you think she's giving them the run around?"

"I don't know, hard to say, but someone is up there."

They stopped talking to listen for the direction that the walking was coming from. Maria pointed to a set of double doors to the right of the staircase. She unholstered her gun. Of course, she didn't really want to point it at a teenager or a homeless person, but also wasn't stupid enough to go ahead empty handed. Anyone could be running around in here, though she didn't know how they could have gone undiscovered with there being a police presence ever since Riley disappeared.

Maria stood outside the double doors. By her side, Frankie nodded, and they both kicked open the doors at the same time.

"Police," hollered Maria, "stay right there where we can see you!"

Maria shone her flashlight around the long, empty ward but could see no one. Frankie did the same on the opposite side. Then they heard a slow, drawn-out shuffling sound as if someone had begun to drag themselves across the floor.

"Where are they?" Frankie hissed at her.

She looked everywhere but still couldn't see anybody. "I don't know."

They took another step forward, flashlights moving quickly over the floor and along the walls. A high-pitched screaming sound pierced the air around them, so loud that Frankie lifted his hands to cover his ears. They spun around to face empty space. The sound of footsteps moved to where the walls were steeped in shadows so black and dense the flashlights didn't penetrate it.

Maria swallowed the lump in her throat. Her fingers trembled as they gripped the gun. She holstered it, not trusting herself to be able to take a good aim at someone in these conditions. At that moment the doors behind them exploded open with such force they slammed into the walls, knocking huge chunks of the damp, rotting plaster to the ground. Then the whole room went still. Not a sound could be heard except for the steady pitter-patter of rain as it hit the wooden boards covering the windows.

"What the hell was that?" Frankie stared at Maria.

She shrugged, trying to appear calm, even though her insides had turned to iced water. "May have been the wind screaming through the holes in the roof. Come on, let's get out of here and check the other rooms out."

He stared at her in disbelief. "If you believe that, you'll believe anything. And you want to carry on?"

"It's why we drove ninety minutes to get here, isn't it? I don't know what is going on but I'm not leaving here until I'm satisfied that the kid isn't hiding or playing pranks on us. Plus, you are the one who threw the whole serial killer hiding place theory into the mix, so now we've got no choice but to double-check. Why were those cops so keen to get away? Don't they think this is the ideal place for an escaped con to hide out in? So, get moving because the longer you hang around here, the longer we're stuck in this goddamn building."

Maria noticed as they left the room that Frankie was no longer loitering behind her but was close to her side. They walked toward a doorway further down the corridor that had police tape across it, flapping in the cool breeze. Was she completely mad not to run out of here? And why hadn't Riley done exactly that? Maria refused to believe a teenage girl could vanish into thin air. Perhaps she'd run away and used her friends as an alibi so she couldn't be found? If so, it was a shitty thing to do to your friends. Maria needed to interview them. She was a good judge of character and was confident she'd know if they were hiding anything.

She shone the flashlight inside the room, which seemed to

be an old treatment room. There was a table in the middle with a bank of broken spotlights above it. An ancient, rusted wheelchair lay on its side. Had it always been that way or had the kids tipped it over? The room was otherwise empty apart from a huge chunk of plaster that had caved in off the ceiling and covered the table in debris.

"Nothing remarkable in here. Let's find the tower."

Frankie didn't reply, so she went to walk away, when he caught hold of the sleeve of her jacket and tugged her backwards. She stared at him, puzzled, and saw that his normally tanned face was ashen. He pointed toward the wheelchair. One wheel spun slowly around. Maria blinked. It hadn't been moving seconds ago. She scanned the room for open windows or holes in the ceiling that a draft could be flowing through but there weren't any. The wheel gathered speed, until it spun around so fast that the spokes began to blur.

Frankie pushed her and hissed, "We need to leave. *Now*."

She shook her head. "No way, not until we've checked out the tower."

"Maria!"

"I thought you liked this sort of thing; you watch those TV shows, you're the expert."

"Yeah, but there's safety in numbers and there are only two of us, and a lot of strange stuff going on in here."

Determined not to let him know that underneath her cool exterior she was terrified, Maria shrugged. "Like I keep saying, it could be past memories imprinted onto the surroundings. Isn't that what they refer to as a residual haunting on the TV?"

"Yeah, but—"

"Christ, Frankie, a kid is missing, and yes, this place is scary but let's do our job." She sounded a lot braver than she felt. "I saw someone up in that tower. If we leave now, then we're not doing what we get paid to do. The local cops have an escaped con. It could be him up there. Someone has to check it out. If you were an escaped con, where would you want to hide?"

"Not here," replied Frankie. "But if it is him, he could be armed and dangerous. Probably hasn't even heard about the missing girl, though. It's barely made the news."

"I don't know whether to be impressed your brain thought of that or pissed that you keep coming up with every excuse to get out of here. Especially when it's your fault we're here in the first place. If he is hiding up there, which, you're right, he'd have to be either foolish or brave to do, we have protection."

She lifted the flap of her jacket and pointed to her gun.

"Ain't gonna help us with any ghosts, though, is it?"

She shook her head and set off toward the stairs, unable to shake the feeling that someone other than Frankie was walking behind her. She could hear the shuffle of feet close to her and told herself it was her imagination running wild.

Arriving on the next floor, with Frankie at her side, she saw that it was in a terrible state. The holes in the roof let in the rain, while the paint on the walls peeled, the stench of damp was heavy and bird crap was plastered everywhere. Even someone who led the shittiest of lives could find a better place to hide out than here. Maria wouldn't stay over in this building for any amount of money. There were fewer doors up here and they were more spread out along the corridor. Maria pushed one open and found what looked like a spacious hotel room, with faded pretty pastel wallpaper blooming with the black flowers of mold. All that was left of the two, likely once comfortable, beds were the box springs.

"Welcome to being wealthy and insane," whispered Frankie.

Maria nodded. "Money isn't everything, but it does buy a lot of comfort."

These days she knew about the comforts of the rich first hand. Harrison lived in the top-floor penthouse apartment of the newly renovated Waldorf Towers, and it was stunning. She'd only visited him a couple of times because he knew how overwhelmed she got when faced with his wealth. He'd take her out on as low-key dates as he could come up with. They'd gone to Coney Island and eaten at Nathan's Hot Dogs on the boardwalk under a burning hot sun with the salty smell of the Atlantic Ocean and fried onions in the air. She'd loved the funfair and Denny's *Wonder Wheel,* although the rickety, old wooden carriage of the fun ride had made her fear her mortality.

She really did like Harrison, but they were just on two different levels. It was funny how he could overlook her being a detective on a moderate income, yet she couldn't push aside the fact that he was a multi-millionaire. Growing up, she'd never felt good enough and had always been afraid of anyone with money. Although she'd fought tooth and nail to get to where she was in her career, this fear still reared its head occasionally, and Harrison Williams seemed to bring all these ugly thoughts to the surface.

Bringing Maria back to the moment, a cool breeze kissed the back of her neck. She jumped and her fingers brushed her skin, finding it cool to the touch. Maria slowly turned around to see where the cold air had come from but there was nothing and no one standing behind her. She waved her hand to see if she could feel a draft.

"Why are you doing hand signals?"

She didn't reply, not sure how to put what had happened into words. It hadn't felt threatening. If anything, it had been a little too intimate.

"Come on," she said, "there must be an access door somewhere."

They were halfway down the corridor when Frankie, who was right behind her again, stopped and turned around.

"I hear footsteps, can you?"

She couldn't hear anything, but she saw how pale his face was and how wide his eyes had become. Again, Maria didn't comment. Despite his bravado, it was clear that Frankie Conroy was not cut out to be a ghost hunter. She strode toward a small door at the very end of the hallway. She wanted to check out the tower and be out of here. Reaching forward she gripped the handle and instantly her fingers recoiled. It felt like a solid block of ice. In case she'd somehow imagined it, she gripped it again, firmer this time. But like before, she had to let go. Her fingers burned as if they'd touched something too cold for too long.

"Ouch."

"What's up?"

"That handle. You have a go."

Frankie rolled his eyes and flexed his bicep. "Step aside for the big guy."

He gripped the door handle then let it go with a yelp.

"Jeez, why is that frozen?" he asked. "It's raining, not snowing."

Frankie tugged down his sleeve and twisted the handle sharply. It didn't move. It was either frozen solid or locked. Maria bent down to look through the keyhole, wondering if she was going to regret this moment for the rest of her life. In the horror movies she'd watched as a teenager, main characters would look through keyholes to see an eyeball or something far worse staring back at them.

Lifting the flashlight, she peered through the hole at the blackness. She couldn't see a thing, but she heard the faintest noise on the other side of the door. Was it breathing? Someone—or something—knew they were there and was waiting for them to enter or leave. She was certain it wasn't a teenage girl in need of help. Maria straightened up.

"I don't think she's up there. It's locked from the outside."

Frankie raised his eyebrows. "Changed your mind? What did you see?"

"Nothing. I saw nothing. It's too dark. Come on, this is a waste of time. We need to go speak to her friends."

Frankie knew better than to argue with Maria when she'd made up her mind. He followed behind as she walked briskly toward the stairs. Maria wasn't going to tell him that she feared something far worse than a missing teenage girl was on the other side of that door. Whatever was hiding in that tower didn't want to come out into the light. And for now, Maria was happy to leave it behind in the darkness.

DECEMBER 1960

Faye Miller opened her eyes. It felt as if they had been stuck together with glue. She stared at the white ceiling above. She was not in her bed at home, that was for sure, and she was chilled to the bone. Tiny goosebumps rose on her arms as she shivered. The ceiling was much higher than hers and the mattress was harder. Her head ached as if she had a hangover, but she didn't remember drinking last night. She didn't remember last night, full stop.

The all-too-familiar feeling of being helpless and out of control set in as she struggled to calm her pounding heart. *Deep breaths, you're alive, you're fine, you're safe.* But where the hell was she? Sitting up, she saw that she wasn't lying on a bed at all. She was on the floor. She turned her head to study the room. Only then did it hit her. She wasn't in a hotel room, not even a cheap motel off the interstate. She was in a padded cell in a hospital for the insane. With this realization, she opened her already parched mouth and screamed until her voice became so hoarse and raspy it was reduced to barely a whisper.

The door to her room was thrown open and a huge guy

dressed in a white orderly uniform stared at her with his arms crossed.

He sniggered. "What's wrong with you? Are you sick?"

Faye stared at him. She knew him. He was the one who'd carried her in here kicking and screaming yesterday afternoon. He'd pinned her down while the nurse gave her a shot in the arm of something that must have knocked her clean out. While she wasn't objectionable to prescription drugs, she preferred to decide to take them herself.

"Let me out of here. This isn't where I'm supposed to be."

Smiling cruelly, he asked, "Where are you supposed to be?"

"Not here. I'm not sick. I'm sad, I'm exhausted and mentally drained. I don't need to be locked up and treated as if I'm nuts because I'm not. Where's my doctor? She will tell you this has all been a huge mistake."

A nurse pushed past him. "Move your ass, Burt." She was tiny compared to his hulking figure blocking out the light and Faye's escape route. She must have been strong because he stumbled to the side at the force of her push.

"Good morning, Faye, how are you?"

Faye eyed the nurse with suspicion, and particularly the silver kidney-shaped tray she was holding. It contained two cups, one filled with an assortment of pills, and another filled with water. She didn't care about the meds, but the sight of the water made her lick her lips. She was so thirsty she could drink a river dry. Whatever they'd pumped her full of yesterday had left her with what felt like the world's worst hangover.

"I want to be let out of here. As I told him, there's been a mistake—I should not be here."

The nurse put her hand on her hip. "Hmm, are you the same Faye Miller who was admitted yesterday by Doctor Friskle? The same Faye Miller who is under strict orders to rest and recuperate?"

Faye thought carefully before answering. Faye Miller was

the name she used whenever she wanted to be left alone, whenever she turned her spotlight off. She had two options, either play along and hope they took her to a private room or lose her shit. She was on the verge of choosing the second option, but she nodded.

"Your doctor thinks you need a complete break from reality. No TV, books, newspapers, magazines. No outside influences. Just time on your own to process your thoughts and feelings."

Faye closed her eyes; she was too tired to fight this. The nurse stepped toward her. "Take your meds like a good girl and I'll get your breakfast."

Faye opened her eyes and glared at the older woman. She was speaking to her in the most patronizing way she'd ever heard, as if she were a child. Despite this, Faye nodded and held out her hand for the small, plastic cup containing God knows what. The bulky orderly watched her every move as if she might attack the nurse at any moment. He needn't bother. She was a lot of things—sad, depressed, lonely, exhausted—but she wasn't a violent person by nature. That wasn't to say that she couldn't or wouldn't defend herself if she needed to.

She tipped the pills into her mouth, pushing them into her cheek and underneath her tongue, and swallowed the water.

"Did you swallow them?"

She stuck her tongue out and the nurse smiled.

"See, all you need to do is let us take care of you for a little while and everything won't seem so bad. I'll go get your breakfast and you can eat it in peace. How lovely that you don't have to do a single thing. Just eat, drink and sleep. I sure wish someone would let me do that for a while—you don't know how lucky you are."

Faye didn't feel so lucky. Out in the hallway someone was howling while another person sobbed uncontrollably. The nurse and orderly left her to it, but not before the orderly turned back and winked at her. She waited until the door was closed then turned to face the wall and spat out the tablets into her cupped hand.

She recognized the small white Phenergan tablets she'd been taking for years, along with Nembutal and a couple of chloral hydrate pills, or Mickey Finns as they were called in the business. They helped her sleep on the nights her mind wouldn't shut down and she usually washed them down with a couple of glasses of champagne. This time she dry-swallowed them, knowing fine well it wasn't enough to knock her out on its own. Years of taking every known medicine meant most prescription drugs didn't have the same effect on her as they did on other people. She looked for a suitable hiding place for the other pills. She wasn't about to put herself into a medical stupor in this hospital where anyone could take advantage of her, and she'd no doubt that they would try, because that happened to her alter ego on a regular basis.

She both loved and hated the life she'd created for herself. The attention she'd craved for so many years—and still did—was now the thing she hated most about it. Could she learn to live with the publicity-seeking monster that lived inside her without losing her mind to it completely? She had to at least try.

It was time to reclaim a little of herself back. To reconnect with the woman who could walk down the street without getting catcalled and ambushed and hadn't appreciated how wonderful that was. To return to the life where photographers didn't hide in bushes to catch you off guard. When she could meet a man who loved her for her and not for some false ideal of a woman who only existed on the big screen. Most of all, she missed having girlfriends she could confide in, go dancing or get a milkshake at the diner with, without worrying that she'd look seven pounds fatter on camera.

A solitary tear rolled down her cheek. She was so lonely and yet she could never end this constant rollercoaster of ups and downs. And lately it was nothing but down, down, down.

FOUR

Frankie slammed the front door behind them both. There was a loud click like a key turning.

"Did the door just lock itself?" He shook his head and turned the handle to check. "This place is far too alive for something that's been abandoned since the seventies."

"That's fine with me. I'm not going back in there." Maria shuddered. "What are we supposed to do, hang around here until Starsky and Hutch get back?"

At that moment, something high above Frankie caught her eye. A black shadow was hurtling out of the window toward the ground. She dived toward him and pushed him out of the way before whatever it was could land on his head. She expected to hear a crash of some kind, but nothing happened. Except Frankie looked as if she'd scared him to death.

"What was that for?"

"I saw something falling."

He looked up doubtfully. "From where?"

Maria shrugged. The only window that wasn't boarded up was the turreted one in the tower.

"Never mind. Must have been a bird swooping down."

He arched an eyebrow at her. "Yeah, whatever you say. Are you losing your mind, Miller?"

She ignored him and walked toward his car, holding herself back from running toward it. The quicker she got away from here, the better she would feel.

Frankie was inside the car before she'd opened the door. Neither said a word as he put the car in reverse and turned around. Frankie drove along the winding drive and through the gates. He kept the engine running as she got out and closed them. All was quiet and still, apart from the sound of the car. No birds, or animals, or traffic.

"Don't blame me, this is our job," he said as she got back in.

"Ten thousand dollars a year extra doesn't cut it. You know that, right?"

He nodded. "I'm starting to."

"Now what? We still don't have the addresses of the kids who were with her."

Maria leaned across to grab the file off the back seat and scanned the papers inside. There was an address for Riley, but not the others.

"Let's head to the local station and get the information we need ourselves. Somebody will be able to help us, surely."

She typed the zip code into her phone and Frankie followed the directions until they reached a red brick building on Municipal Plaza. There wasn't a single police vehicle parked outside.

"Looks like there's nobody home," Frankie said once they were parked.

"Someone must be manning the phones. Didn't your friend mention somebody called Dorothy?"

They entered the reception area. On a notice board, beside an assortment of wanted posters, was a much bigger poster of Riley Holt's smiling face. Frankie pressed the buzzer on the wall, and they waited to see if anyone was home.

"Can I help you?"

Maria turned to see a small grey-haired woman with thick-rimmed black spectacles on a pretty gold chain around her neck. She smiled, but Maria thought the woman looked tired. If she were her boss, she would send her home to get some rest. She smiled back at her.

"Ma'am, we're Detectives Conroy and Miller. We're here to assist with the search for Riley Holt."

"You're the city cops who deal with the weird stuff?"

Frankie looked a little caught off guard, so Maria stepped in.

"We deal with unusual cases, yes, that's us."

Dorothy nodded. "That's good because there is nothing straightforward about this. God bless her, Riley is such a good girl. Such a lovely, kind girl. She would not worry us all like this by choice. Why don't you come through to the back and I'll get you something to drink?"

She opened the side door to the back office. The walls were painted a bland yellow color that reminded Maria of runny eggs. Dorothy pointed to two chairs.

"Take a load off. What can I get you?"

Frankie shook his head. He was a coffee snob and wouldn't drink instant.

"We're okay, thanks." Maria smiled. "It's Dorothy, isn't it?"

"That's me. Despatcher, general office manager and chief coffee maker."

"Any luck with the escaped prisoner?"

"There has been a sighting at one of the outbuildings on Ned Jones' old farmstead. They're all out there running around chasing their tails when he'll be holed up in that barn. I suppose it's what they get paid to do. I suspect he's not the brightest though if he's hiding so close to town, be back in lock up just in time for supper at this rate. Makes the general public feel safer if they see cops all over the place, even if they don't know what they're doing."

Maria smiled at her. "Would you happen to have the addresses of Riley's friends who were with her? I need to talk to them."

"I have their statements out back if you want a copy?"

"Yes, that would be helpful. Thank you. Do you know any of them, personally?"

Dorothy nodded. "I know Drew and Ryan. Not Noah so much. He doesn't come here with Riley after school, but the others often trail along with her."

"Does she come here often after school?"

"Her daddy is the chief. She comes here most days to get a key, or to meet him for supper if he's working late. Her mom left a couple of years ago."

Maria glanced at Frankie. "Where did she go?"

Dorothy shrugged. "Ran away with that fool, Curtis, from the 7-Eleven. The pair of them took off like a couple of lovesick teenagers. Damn near broke the chief's heart, and Riley was devastated to find her momma left her for a guy not much older than herself."

"How did the chief take that?" Maria asked.

"Every which way a man whose wife runs out on him would. Angry, sad, depressed, guilty."

Maria wondered if Riley had run away to find her mom. Maybe the chief wasn't a good father, or maybe she just wanted to see her mother again and didn't want to upset him.

"Do you know where they went, her mother and Curtis?"

Dorothy, with spectacles perched on the end of her nose, peered at her.

"Nobody knows. It's like they disappeared off the face of the earth. I guess if you don't want to be found, then it can be done."

"Could Riley have gone to see them?"

She shrugged. "Look, I'm just the general dogsbody. I don't

know whether she would even want to see her mother again. She was pretty mad at her for walking out." She paused. "Let me go get those statements for you and you can ask her friends yourself. They'll know more than me. But I can tell you now that I don't believe she would put her daddy through this heartbreak again, having watched him fall apart in front of her. That isn't the kind of girl she is. She's more like the chief than she was ever like her momma."

Dorothy left and neither Maria nor Frankie spoke, but judging by the look on Frankie's face Maria could tell they were thinking the same thing. There were two distinct possibilities. Either Riley Holt ran away to find her mother, or she was stuck in that old asylum somewhere. Maria also had to consider the possibility that the chief's wife and her lover might not have actually run away. If no one had heard from them since, something might have happened to them. Had Riley discovered what that was and been silenced? Dorothy came back in with some xeroxed reports, passing a sheaf of papers to each of them.

"Got you both a copy of their witness reports and addresses."

"Thank you, Dorothy," Frankie said. "Now, if you were us, who would you go visit first out of these kids?"

"Drew, for sure. If Riley had any secrets, it would be Drew she'd share them with."

Frankie smiled at her. "What time does the chief finish? We're going to need to speak to him, too."

"He should have finished two hours ago, but he won't go home. Not while his daughter is missing and there's a fugitive at large. Between you and me, he hasn't been home at all since Riley disappeared. He's sleeping on the sofa in his office. He thinks I don't know but I do."

They stood up, and Maria thanked her again. "We'll be seeing you around."

Dorothy nodded. "You certainly will."

Outside, as they got back in the car, Maria knew exactly what Frankie was going to say.

"So," he said, "what about the chief's wife and her lover, then? Don't you think it's a bit strange they disappeared, and no one seems to be bothered where the hell they are?"

"I do think it's very strange, and I think people are probably ignoring warning signs because he's the chief. You think he killed them both and Riley found out? He could have killed her, too, and made it look like she disappeared?"

Frankie let out a long, drawn-out sigh that made Maria feel tired just listening to it. "I suppose he could have, but that doesn't explain the weird stuff in that old hospital, does it? And don't deny it, Maria, you couldn't get out of there quick enough."

"Damn it. Why are you so good at reading me?"

He laughed and shook his head. "How about the fact that your eyes were wide open, your hair practically stood on end, and you looked so scared I thought you might crap your pants?"

She gave him the middle finger. "And here was me trying to be nice." She rifled through the sheaf of papers until she found the one with *DREW DEAN* printed at the top. "She lives on the corner of Maddison Avenue and Judson Street. I think we should speak to the guys first though, before she has a chance to warn them we are on our way."

"Fine by me."

They found Noah at home with his mom, though he told them nothing of any use. He was quiet, keeping his eyes downcast the entire time. It was a painful interview. Ryan was much more talkative, but he also didn't give them anything other than the scant information that was already in the reports. When they left his house and got back into the car Maria leaned forwards and typed the zip code into the satnav for Drew's house.

"Let's hope she's a lot more talkative than those two—what a waste of time that was."

Nodding, Frankie pulled out the lot. Maria knew they were thinking the same thing. There had to be more to this than the kids were admitting because of who Riley's dad was.

FIVE

The pale green house on the corner of Maddison Ave and Jutson Street had lights on in every window yet no cars were parked outside.

Frankie shook his head. "Goddamn kids, burning every light whilst the parents are out working their ass off to pay for it."

"Or she could be scared of the dark after the other night?"

Frankie seemed unsure. "Maybe."

"Let me do the talking, okay? Don't be some hard ass on the kid. She's been through enough."

He gave a look of total innocence. "Would I ever?"

But Maria was already out of the car. She knocked on the door, despite knowing that they should really wait to speak with Drew until her parents were home. Plus, for all they knew, they might just not have owned a car. A radio must have been on somewhere inside the house, as Maria could hear the faint chatter of a DJ in the background.

"Who is it?" The sudden, cautious voice on the other side of the door surprised her. She hadn't heard footsteps.

"Detectives Miller and Conroy from the 6th Precinct."

"Where's that?" The voice sounded younger than Maria had expected.

"Manhattan."

The door slowly opened and a red-eyed teenager wearing sweats and with her chestnut hair in a messy bun stared at them. "Why are you here?"

"I think you know why, Drew. We need to talk to you about Riley."

Drew held out her hand expectantly and Maria raised her badge. Frankie did the same.

"Are you here on your own? We really need to speak to you."

Drew shook her head. "My grampa is out back."

"Do you want to go ask him if it's okay for us to come inside?"

Drew glanced from Maria to Frankie, bit her bottom lip and opened the door. The girl looked terrified. It made Maria uneasy that she was letting them into her home with so little resistance. Walking inside, they were met with the smells of lemon furniture polish and chili. They followed her to the kitchen where, sure enough, a big pot of chili was bubbling on the stovetop.

Frankie nodded appreciatively. "Now that smells good. Did you make it?"

Drew stirred, turned to him and smiled. "Grampa's secret recipe. Only he knows it."

"And it's going to stay that way until the day I croak it. Now, can I get you folks a drink? Why don't you take a load off and tell me who you are and why you're calling so late in the day?"

Grampa wasn't quite as old as Maria had imagined, perhaps in his late sixties. He'd a thick head of snowy white hair and pale blue eyes that crinkled at the corner. He crossed the room to Drew, gave her a hug, then let her go. Even in their brief embrace Maria could see the genuine warmth and love the girl had for him.

"We're detectives from the 6th Precinct."

"Is that Greenwich Village? You came all the way here to speak to Drew about her friend Riley? I guess the chief is calling in all the favors. Can't say that I blame him. God forbid, if it was Drew who had gone missing in that place, I'd be camped out there trying to find her. I'm Abraham Dean, you've already met my granddaughter, Drew Dean."

Frankie intervened. "I'm Frankie and this is Maria. Actually, the chief has no idea that we're here. It was one of his deputies, an old friend of mine, who called us."

"And you came running just like that? Imagine."

Maria looked at Drew. "We deal with things that are a little unusual. Are your parents around, Drew?"

Drew stared back, eyes wide, and asked, "What do you mean, unusual?" She looked at the floor. "And no, my parents are dead. They died in a car wreck two years ago."

"I'm sorry to hear that. It must be so hard for you." Maria paused. Drew nodded, and she continued, "To answer your question, we deal with crimes that don't seem to be the norm, strange things that are hard to explain, that kind of stuff. Can you tell me what really happened inside that old hospital, Drew?"

Drew glanced at her grampa, and he gave her a nod of encouragement. Maria realized then that the girl had already told him. She glanced at Maria for the briefest of moments, as if trying to read her, and then lowered her head.

"You're not gonna believe me."

"Try me. We've both seen things that would make your hair go white and give you sleepless nights for the rest of your life. Is that what happened to you, Drew, inside that hospital? Did you see something that scared you so bad you couldn't tell the chief?

Or was there a person in there and you got scared they may have hurt Riley? Which is it?"

Tears welled in the girl's eyes, and Maria felt bad for pushing her, but she needed to know the full story. There wasn't nearly enough information on the report they'd been handed at the station. She was certain there was so much more going on than what Drew had told the local officers.

"I read that Riley got separated from the others. Then you found her, and you were pretending to be a patient. You heard a noise out in the hallway, got scared and you all ran, except for Riley who didn't follow you out."

Drew nodded.

"How did you get separated in the beginning?"

"She found some old books. Riley loves to read, and she was looking at them for a while, and when she realized she was alone, she couldn't find us. She said she ended up in an empty ward where there was a fire that had gone out."

Maria glanced over at Frankie. Was this proof that someone was hiding out in that place? "You left your friend alone?"

"It wasn't my fault. I was terrified once we got inside and not paying attention."

"Okay, so would you normally leave your friend alone in a strange place?"

Drew shook her head. "No way. We've done this kind of thing before. Not in the asylum, but empty buildings, and we always stick close together. We've never left any of us on our own, not once."

"Why do you like exploring old buildings?"

She shrugged. "The guys like it more than me and Riley, but yeah, it's fun. Or it used to be."

Maria smiled at her. "I need you to be totally honest with me about what happened next. I'm not here to judge you. I don't want anything other than the truth. If we're going to find Riley, I need that, not some fudged up, sweetened version of it. I know it must have been hard talking to Riley's dad, but we're not here to shout at you, okay? We're here to help and bring your friend home where she belongs. Can you do that?"

Drew gulped and nodded. Maria reached out and took hold of her hand, squeezed it once then let go. After a moment, Drew went on.

"Riley said she thought she heard footsteps upstairs above her, and voices. She thought it was us, but when she got up there, into this big, dark old ward, it seemed like there was nobody inside. She turned to leave but there was someone standing on the other side of the door. Riley said she couldn't see their face, but they had this long, straggly hair and their head was bent so far forwards she thought their neck was deformed or something. When she told us, I thought it might be a homeless person."

She stopped talking and Maria felt cold fingers of fear creeping up her spine. It sounded very much as if Drew was describing the College Kid Killer, who she'd seen in photographs online. Did Drew know about him? Maria doubted she was old enough to remember the case, unless she was into true crime.

"Did she agree with you about it being a homeless person, or did she think it was somebody else?"

"She said it looked like a patient from when the place was open. I don't know why as the hospital has been closed for decades."

"Have you ever heard of Malcolm Collins?"

Drew shook her head. "No, who is he?"

"A terrible guy, who got arrested at the hospital in the early aughts. I wouldn't recommend looking him up. Then what happened?"

"Riley said this person disappeared. She heard us calling her name, looked up and they'd gone. Then she went out and found us. The really weird thing was, as she described him, I could really picture him in my mind. And as I was walking down the corridor, I couldn't stop feeling as if whatever or whoever it was had snuck up on me and was following me somehow, even though I couldn't see them. It was so creepy."

Maria had felt the same way inside that hospital. She waited for Drew to continue.

"We found an old treatment room. There was this horrible chair in there, like when you go to the orthodontist, and I was messing around on it. I guess I was showing off to the guys and I feel so bad that I did that now. I didn't know people had actually died in there. Riley told me to stop it, said I shouldn't be disrespectful to the dead, and then a piece of the ceiling fell down and hit me on the head. It cut me."

"How badly were you injured?" Maria was wondering if the girl could have been concussed and if so, was the story she was telling them the truth? It all sounded so far-fetched although she had experienced strange things, too. They would need to speak to the other two to see if their stories corroborated.

"Just a small cut on my forehead. It bled a little, not a lot. Then the room got so cold we could see our breath in front of us. The air smelled bad, too, like something gone off. I looked into the corner and thought I saw a black shape; well, it was more of a shadow, but it was moving and getting bigger. We all got scared and ran out of there, only we didn't know which way to go and had to turn back on ourselves. It was dark and I was terrified that whatever was in that room would get us. Then we realized that Riley wasn't with us. We went back to look for her, but it still smelled awful and the wheel on a chair began to spin. We were so scared and ran until we were clambering back out of the window to get outside. We all piled out... except for Riley."

Frankie stared at Drew with horror etched across his face. He was always so good at empathizing with victims.

"We went back to look for Riley... I mean, we were scared of going back but we had to. She is my friend. I thought she was right behind Ryan when we ran. I never would have left her if I'd known."

She began to cry, big sobs, and her grampa stood up, wrapped his arms around her, and shushed her as he rocked her.

"I'm sorry, Drew," Maria said gently, "you must have been so scared."

She nodded. "I can't stop thinking about her. She's stuck in that place somewhere, I know it. That thing, whatever it was, it took her."

"Now, I have to ask. Do you think Riley could have planned it, so she could run away to go be with her mom? Leaving you all thinking she was lost in the hospital?"

Drew looked up at Maria. She wiped her eyes with the sleeve of her sweater and shook her head.

"No, why would she want to do that? She hates her mom. She took off with that guy and never even told her where she was going. Left her dad in a bad way and Riley said she'd never speak to her ever again. She wouldn't pretend to be lost someplace so she could go have a week with her mom. We tell each other everything. She would have said if she was going to do that."

Drew's grampa stood up. "Hey, now. My granddaughter is upset enough. How about we take a break and eat? I'm starving and I bet you could do with something hot to warm your bellies, if you drove all the way from the Village to come here."

Frankie grinned. "Boy, I thought you'd never ask."

Maria glared at him. She didn't want to sit here and eat chili. She wanted to go speak to the chief and the two boys. But she knew that Frankie with an empty stomach was more hard work than he was worth, so she smiled politely.

"That's very kind of you."

Grampa beamed. "You are in for a treat. You've never tasted

anything this good before. Drew, get me some dishes and the butter."

Drew did as she was asked, and before long they were eating bowls of chili and rice, mopping it up with richly buttered bread. Maria had to admit it—she hadn't tasted anything so good in a long time. Grampa got three cold bottles of Bud out of the fridge. Uncapping them, he passed them to Frankie and Maria.

"Drew, do you want one?"

She shook her head, so he gave her a can of cola.

"Now, I've been thinking a lot these past couple of days about that place. I haven't been inside it for years, but it always scared the crap out of me when I worked there as a groundsman."

Drew stared at him. "You never told me you worked there."

He shrugged. "I don't think about it. It was long before your time, kiddo, and I didn't want to make you more interested in that place. Everyone knows what teenagers are like—you tell them no and they go do it anyway."

Maria sipped at the beer. She didn't really want it but didn't want to appear rude either, unlike Frankie who'd almost downed his bottle in one mouthful.

"Did you check the grounds? They're expansive. I'm assuming you've been there for a look around."

She shook her head. "It was getting dark, so we only looked inside."

"There's an old cemetery in the grounds, must be overgrown now, and badly neglected. I used to tend to those graves the best I could. Never knew who was inside them, just rows of wooden crosses that were nailed together in the old woodwork shop. I always thought it was mighty cruel of the staff to make the patients craft their own grave markers. If they were lucky, they'd get a number scratched into it, but more often than not, the deceased would be buried in a hole with one of those wonky, wooden crosses put on top. Sad, that's all there was to remember them by. No relatives to visit or bring them flowers. I did my best and laid flowers when I could, but you know I'd get in trouble with the nurse in charge if she caught me. She was an old hag. She seemed to dislike her job and the people she was supposed to take care of. I mean, I wasn't overjoyed having to dig graves—it was never on the job description, but you did what you were told, no questions asked. I imagine the chief has had those grounds turned upside down, but you never know."

He stopped talking as he noticed the expression on Drew's face.

"Thanks for telling us," Maria said. "We'll go check out the grounds first thing and we'll speak to the chief, too."

"Good luck with that one. He's rolling round town like a loaded gun. I don't know why the guy doesn't take some time off, stay home."

Frankie shrugged. "I guess it's a hard one to call. I don't think I'd be able to go home and do nothing if it was my kid out there."

Grampa nodded. "No, you're right. Of course, he's going to be heartsick with worry. I just have a bad feeling about that place. I've always had a bad feeling about it. I was so mad with Drew when she said she'd been inside there, and now Riley is missing." He'd turned to look at his granddaughter. "I've warned you so many times not to go there."

Drew looked as if she was going to cry, and her grandfather reached for her hand. "I'm not mad, honey. It's just a bad place. The sooner they knock it down the better. It needs someone to go in and bless the ground it's built on. They should get a shaman to come in and do their thing. Lord knows what that hospital was built on in the first place. The whole area belonged to the Wappinger."

Maria's mind was working overtime. Native American

tribal land, hidden cemeteries, serial killers, shadow figures and a missing teenager didn't make for a good mix.

Frankie finished the last of his beer and stood, blotting his mouth on a piece of kitchen paper that he tore from the roll on the table. "Thank you, Drew, and thanks for the delicious chili, Abraham. It was wonderful."

"I'll see you folks out, whilst Drew clears up." Abraham winked at his granddaughter, and she groaned, but began to clear the table.

"She's a good kid," he told Maria and Frankie, on their way to the front door. "Been through a terrible time when my son and his wife died. I've been on my own for years after my own good wife Laurie passed with the cancer, so it was a bit of a shock having a teenager come to live with me. I know she's telling the truth. Whether you choose to believe her or not is up to you, but there has always been something dark lurking in that hospital. The nurses used to tell stories in the staff room about a shadow that would appear in patients' rooms when they were near to death. It scared the crap out of me. I only went inside for meals and coffee breaks. I don't know how the rest of the staff could work in there, especially the night staff."

"What do you think happened to Riley," Maria asked, "off the record?"

He seemed to consider whether to share his real opinion. "I think it's possible that thing has been lurking in there for years. It saw an opportunity and took it. Four kids messing around in a place they had no business being. It was never going to let them all leave without taking one."

"But take them where exactly?"

He shrugged. "I couldn't tell you. Does it have a lair, does it collect souls, take them to hell, take them to another world? Who knows? But I'm telling you now, I don't think you're going to find Riley anytime soon, unless you can figure out what that thing wants and how to stop it."

Maria sighed. “But what if a person is behind all this?”

Abraham shrugged. “Be a hell of a lot easier to deal with if it was, don’t you think?” He clamped his hand on to Maria’s elbow and squeezed gently. “What I do know is that you should take great care when you go inside that place. Don’t split up, ever. Stay in twos so you can protect each other. You can ignore my warning as the ramblings of an old, crazy guy, and I won’t blame you one little bit. But truthfully, I think there are some things best left alone. And that old hospital is one of them.”

DECEMBER 1960

Faye slept on and off. There wasn't much else to do in a padded room with no TV or even a picture window to stare out of. She knew it was morning by the watery light pooling through the tiny window that was so high up the wall she'd need a ten-foot ladder to reach it. A key turned in the lock and the door opened. She was so sad that she didn't have the energy to move and see who it was.

"Good morning, honey. How are we today?"

This was a much softer, kinder voice than yesterday and she turned her head to see who was speaking. The nurse standing there looked a lot like her dear friend Ella Fitzgerald. They shared the same warm smile that reached their eyes.

"I'm okay, I think," said Faye, sitting up. "Good morning."

The nurse entered the room, pushing the door closed behind her. "Look at you. Why have they got you in here, Miss Miller? You should be up on the second floor. Let me see what I can do to get you moved out of here."

"You would do that, to help me?"

The nurse lowered her voice. "Honey, I read your notes. To be honest, I already know far too much about you from those gutter rags that would sell their own mama to get a story. Let me give you some advice. Don't put up any more fights, and I'll tell my colleagues you're feeling much better and are ready for a change of scenery. Damn, they shouldn't have put you in here. This place makes me so mad at times."

Faye felt hot tears prick at her eyes. It was so long since someone had been this nice to her and expected nothing in return.

"I won't, I promise. What's your name?"

"Dolores, honey. My, you are truly beautiful. Even in this hellhole you're a natural beauty."

Now Faye felt her cheeks burn as well as her eyes water.

"Now, listen up, miss, we haven't got long before that big lout of an orderly comes to see what's going on. You try and stay calm, even though it must be mighty hard. I'd be like a raging bull if they'd slammed me in here for no reason. If he comes in, don't make eye contact, he likes the challenge. Just keep looking at the floor or your hands. It's not right and it's not fair, but he's the head doctor's nephew so he gets away with a lot more than he ought to. I'm going straight up to speak with the big guy himself and get you moved. It may take a couple of hours, so please be patient, but know that I have not forgotten about you, and I am going to do my damn best to make it happen. Have you been taking the pills?"

Faye shook her head. "Some of them. I'm kind of used to a lot of them anyway."

Dolores passed her a plastic cup and some water. "Take what you need and give the rest to me. I'll flush them down the sluice."

Faye picked out the ones she knew would help to clear her head and passed the rest back.

"Thank you. I really appreciate you being so kind to me."

It was Dolores' turn for tears. "My pleasure, Miss Miller. I've been saying for a long time that I'd love to give you some good, old country loving and show you how admired you are. If I can help you, I will do everything in my power to do so, but this is between you and me, okay? I hate this place, but I can't leave the patients. They'd have nobody to fight their battles and show them how much they matter in this world."

Faye crossed the room and hugged Dolores for the briefest of moments.

"Dolores, you are an angel and when I get out of here, I'll make sure everyone knows how wonderful you are."

The nurse laughed. "Get away with you. I'm just following the path God saw fit to put me on, Miss Miller."

"Well, lucky for me that you crossed mine. And you call me Faye. I'm in need of a friend, and you are perfect."

Dolores took the pill cup from her and tipped the remaining tablets into her pocket. "Who'd have thought that big, old Dolores would be friends with Faye Miller? Now that makes my heart sing! Whenever you're feeling all sad, you remember me. I am here to give you hugs whenever you need them."

With a wink, she left the room, locking the door behind her. Faye thought that the world needed more people like Dolores in it. People who were kind meant everything. She knew that more than anything after the past few years spent in the cutthroat world of movie stardom, where everyone wanted a piece of you but gave nothing back in return.

It didn't take long for Dolores to return. At least, it didn't seem like much time had passed before she appeared in the doorway along with the rude guy. He wasn't grinning at Faye today and he hung back behind Dolores. Faye saw from his body language that he was scared of the nurse, which made her feel even better.

"I have some great news for you, Miss Miller. You're off to the second floor, which is where you should have gone in the first place, but never mind. You'll be just fine when we get you up there and bathed. Don't mind Burt. He's just here because he's got nothing better to do. Ain't that the truth, Burt?"

Burt glared at her but didn't speak. Dolores smiled at Faye. "Got to earn his money somehow. Come on, honey, let's get you cleaned up and feeling more like yourself."

Faye took her hand, marveling at how soft Dolores' skin was, and how gently she held her.

"Now, don't mind the patients down here. They are a lot more poorly than you are and can say some not very nice things, but we don't take any of it to heart. They don't mean it. They just don't know how to act any different."

Faye followed Dolores out into the corridor, where there were three more rooms with doors like the one she'd just left, and eight cells which looked like they belonged in a prison. A man or woman was pressed up against the bars of each cell.

"Woo wee, can I get a kiss?" came a deep, gravelly voice from one cell.

"Can I get your autograph, miss? Please, I love you so much," a woman called to her, and Faye smiled at them both, turning on that big, Hollywood smile she was famous for.

"Oh my, look who it is. Why are you down here with us nuts? Are you nuts, too? Did you get sick in the head like the rest of us?"

Dolores guided her by the elbow along the corridor to the open doorway at the end. Faye heard Burt growling at the patients to shut up, and then the door was slammed shut, drowning out their shouts. Faye felt sick. How could they think she was like those poor lost souls?

Maybe they were right. Was she losing her mind? Had she ever even been a movie star, or was it all inside her head? Panic began to suck the air out of her chest and as if sensing that she was struggling, Dolores wrapped an arm around her waist and whispered, "You're okay, Miss Miller. Take some deep breaths.

You'll be okay once we get you up to that second floor and into a nice hot bath."

She did as Dolores told her, inhaling through her nose and out through her mouth, until she found herself in an open hallway that looked like the entrance of the Beverly Hills Hotel. A beautiful crystal chandelier hung above the semicircular reception desk where two nurses watched her every move. She didn't look at them but noted the huge double-glass front doors a little ahead of it. She didn't remember being brought in through those. A woman in a smart suit with a small suitcase stood with a nervous-looking man Faye assumed was her husband. She certainly hadn't been booked in like that. Keeping her head down, she followed Dolores to a lift. The doors opened, and they stepped inside. Burt made to follow, and Dolores held out her hand.

"I don't need your assistance now, Burt. You run along and see who does. Thank you."

He scowled at the nurse, who didn't give him a second look. She wasn't remotely intimidated by him and his huge size. When the doors slid shut, she turned to Faye and smiled.

"That man is a walking liability and he's not allowed on the second floor in case he upsets the patients. Now, let me see." She looked Faye up and down. "You look better already." She pulled her into a tight hug. Faye hugged her back and let the woman rock her from side to side before she let her go. "I'm getting you released from here as soon as I can. Can I ask you a favor, though, while we're getting you sorted?"

Faye nodded. "Anything."

"There's a kid up here. She's lost, afraid and scared of her own shadow. She was down where you were, but I got her moved up here. Technically she should be on a ward, not in one of the suites but no one knows how she got here, or even her name. There are no notes on her, so I persuaded the good doctor to treat her like royalty in case she's a spy or someone from the government. I don't think she is. I think she's here by mistake but she's so shell-shocked and traumatized that she hasn't spoken a word since we found her wandering the hallway two nights ago, crying and screaming."

"What do you want me to do?"

"Talk to her if you can. You have a gentle voice, a soothing voice. You might be able to get her to open up a little. I want to get her home to her family, but I can't if we don't know who she is."

Faye nodded. "Of course. How will I know her?"

"She's in the room next door. We don't lock these rooms on the second floor, so she's free to move around, but she hasn't left her room. She just keeps staring down at the gardens and crying. I thought maybe she might talk to you. I understand if you don't want to. I'm being selfish by asking you to do it, but I'm worried about her. The clothes she's wearing are odd. Her shoes, for instance. She arrived wearing only one of them, a red sneaker, but she don't look like any basketball player. I'll catch you later, Miss Miller."

Faye's interest was piqued. She wandered to the large window covered with metal bars to look down onto the grounds that were covered with a dusting of snow. The trees in the woods were nothing but bare branches apart from some of the fir trees mixed in amongst the others. She could do with something to take her mind off this place, and this may just be the thing. She knew that Dolores was being astute in giving her a project, something to make the time pass faster, and she'd never felt such love for a person she'd only just met. The woman was an angel, and when she got out of there, she would see to it that she was recognized for her kindness to people who really needed it.

SIX

They sat in the car. It was fully dark now and there was no way in hell Maria was going back to search the grounds of that hospital. This case was far more complicated than she'd imagined. Give her a dead body any day. At least then they would have something to work with, as sad as it was. Not that she wanted to have to work Riley Holt's murder, but this case was stretching her realm of capability—and what she believed was possible.

"You think Abraham's telling the truth?" she asked Frankie. "About the stories the nurses used to tell?"

"I think so. You saw his face. I would guess there's something lurking in that building that is older than the pair of us, and probably a lot scarier than you without your face on."

Maria gently slapped his arm. "Yeah, I thought so, too. We should speak to some local paranormal experts, find out if anyone has done any legitimate ghost hunts in there. Maybe a historian who could give us a bit more background than the internet searches. I also need to do a full background check on Malcolm Collins. And I want to know who the escaped prisoner is. What if he shared a cell at some point with Malcolm, and he liked the sound of what he was in for?"

"But first we see the chief."

She didn't answer. He was right, but she didn't fancy a fight with some small-town police chief with a huge grudge on his shoulder. Frankie drove them back to the station in the hope that by now he might have returned, and parked next to a police cruiser that hadn't been there earlier.

"Hey, are we driving home after this or sleeping in the car?"

Maria looked at him, horrified. "I am not sleeping in this car with you, especially not in an enclosed space after you've eaten a mountain of chili."

He laughed his deep, loud laughter that she loved so much. A loud knock on the window to the side of her made them both jump. She unrolled the window to a well-built, very tall man in a uniform.

"Can I help you folks?"

"We're looking for Chief Holt."

"Well, you found him. And you are?"

"Detectives Miller and Conroy from the 6th Precinct."

He peered past Maria to take in Frankie, who was no longer laughing.

"Dorothy told me there were two city detectives in town. Why don't you come inside, and we can talk?"

"That would be great, thanks." Maria smiled and it wasn't returned. She couldn't imagine how she'd be feeling if she was in his shoes. Probably pissed with the entire universe and not in the mood for polite conversation. They followed him into the station, where there was no sign of Dorothy, down to the end of the corridor and into his office.

"Take a seat. Can I get you anything?"

"No, thank you, we're good."

They sat down and waited for him to sit behind the old cherrywood desk that was littered with police reports and coffee cups.

"We're sorry about your daughter. Is there any news?"

He shook his head. "Diddly squat. I keep drawing a blank. All I know is that she went into that godforsaken hospital and never came out. Now, kindly tell me what you're doing on my patch when I don't remember inviting you."

Frankie spoke. "I went to the academy with Denny Walker. He phoned me to say he was worried about the whereabouts of your daughter and would we be able to come down and take a look."

"Why would Denny think you could help?"

Frankie side-eyed Maria, and she took over. "We've both been detectives for a long time. Last year we got caught up in a homicide that wasn't your usual murder. There was a sacrifice in the attic of a brownstone where, for want of a better word, a demon had been summoned."

She watched the chief's face go from shock to disbelief to anger.

"And what has that got to do with Riley? Because as far as I know she's not dead."

"No, of course not, but she's missing, in a hospital that is reportedly haunted. We've spoken to her friend Drew and there are some things you might not be fully aware of."

The chief leaned forward. His hands clasped together on the desk in front of him. "Such as?"

"Drew said all of them saw a black shadow figure in the room they were messing around in. It got bigger, and they got scared and ran. That was the last time they saw Riley."

"Did she now? Trying to get herself out of the mess those damn kids made. They dragged my girl into that building then left without her. What a load of crap. She also told me Riley saw a person inside there, too, but we didn't find any trace of them."

"You said yourself your daughter went into that building and never came out. How is that possible when I'm assuming you and your team have searched it inside and out?"

"Of course, we searched it many times over and sent the dogs in."

"Did you search the tower?"

"No, we couldn't get into it. It was bolted from the outside. Riley couldn't have gone up there and locked it after herself. Impossible."

"Someone could have locked it after her though?"

He shrugged. "I shouted until my voice went hoarse. I shouted through the keyhole. If she was up there, she'd have made a noise."

Maria swallowed the lump in her throat. "I'm sorry to say this, but what if she was unable to make a noise?"

Fear filled the chief's eyes. "God damn it, I know you're right. We need to get into that tower. We tried to break the door down. It must be metal, covered in wood or some kind of security door."

"Is there a caretaker for the place? Someone who might have a key for it?"

"Sammi Jo Thompson is the caretaker. She gave us the keys the first night we searched for Riley."

"Did you ask her for the key to the tower?"

Without responding, he picked up the phone and dialed. "Hey, it's the chief. Sammi, did you give me a key for the tower?"

He put the phone onto speaker so they could hear her reply.

"I gave you all the keys I have."

"What about the tower? Do you have keys for that?"

"It should have been on the keyring with the others. Hold on, let me check."

The line went silent. They could hear her moving around in the background.

"Damn it, Duane, I'm sorry. It must have come loose, it's here. I'm on my way, I'll meet you at the hospital."

The chief dropped the phone back into its cradle. "You guys

better come with me. I'm not going to be responsible for my actions if I find my girl hurt in that tower."

Maria glanced at Frankie. Neither of them wanted to go into that place this late at night, but they weren't going to say that.

The chief shrugged on his jacket. "It's gonna be cold in there. Is that all you have to wear?"

Maria looked down at her suit jacket. Frankie was wearing only a light jacket, too. "Poor planning on our side."

They followed the chief down the corridor, stopping by a room full of uniforms and equipment.

"I have to keep this place locked up because my deputies can't behave when it comes to spare kit." He came out with two Beacon PD fleece jackets and two matching, fleece-lined hats with ear flaps, passing them across. Maria took one and pulled it on, glad of the extra warmth. Frankie did the same.

"Thanks, chief. This is kind of you."

"Call me Duane, and you're welcome. I figured if you guys have come all this way to help me find my sweet girl then you can't be all bad. Even if you do sound like you're batshit crazy."

She grinned at him, and he smiled back. Maria realized he must be quite the catch around here now his wife was out of the picture, with his blond, slightly too long hair, blue eyes and bronzed skin, the kind you get from being an outdoor sporty type and not from hours on a tanning bed.

She let Frankie get in the front of the cruiser with the chief —she was happy to sit in the back and let the guys get on with it. She might be a tough city cop but out here where there were open fields and abandoned mental asylums, she felt a little out of her comfort zone.

"Hey, did you catch the escaped con?" Frankie asked as they drove to the hospital.

"Not yet, but it's only a matter of time. He's either holed up somewhere or got a ride out of the county. Hoping for the latter. Takes the heat off me and my department."

"What's he called and what was he in for?"

"Danny Briggs, in for armed robbery. Fool tried to hold up the gas station with a pellet gun."

"Is he dangerous?"

"Maybe. I don't know him myself. It was a couple of towns over. Think he's a regular in lockup for drunken brawling. Who knows what a man is capable of when he's not thinking straight?"

He didn't sound like the kind of perp who would go from bar fights and armed robbery to abduction and murder. "Did you check if he headed toward the hospital?"

"He won't have gone there, not unless he was desperate. I take it you guys have been inside?"

"Yes, we had a look around. Your escaped con, did he have anything to do with Malcolm Collins whilst he was incarcerated?"

"The College Kid Killer? Not that I know of." He paused. "And before you ask, Malcolm Collins is dead, which is about the best place he could be. If you guys went inside, then you'll know it's not the kind of place anyone would want to spend time in of their own free will." His voice caught in the back of his throat, and Maria felt for him.

"It must be so hard, not knowing where she is."

"Riley is a good girl. She would never run away. I know what folks are saying, that she's run off to see her mom, but when Louisa left, she didn't just leave me, she left Riley and it hurt her deep. Some wounds never heal, and it doesn't matter how old you are, being abandoned by your own mom is not something that you can gloss over with a bit of sticky glue to hold the edges together. She hurt me, too, but I'm an adult, not a teenage girl with hormones running wild. After she left, I probably started drinking a little too much, but Riley... she carried on as normal. Still cried herself to sleep most nights. It broke my heart listening to her sobs."

Frankie gave a sympathetic smile. "It's not easy. I found my wife cheating on me with my brother. We haven't got kids thankfully, she never wanted them. I did the same, began drinking a little too much. I'm lucky though, I have Maria to bust my balls on a daily basis."

Duane laughed. "I kept it together as much as I could for Riley, but I could have done with a Maria. Are you two a couple out of work?"

Maria laughed. "God no, we're good friends and great partners. We like to keep it that way."

She noticed that Frankie didn't answer, and she felt guilty. She knew he liked her a lot more than he should do, but she would not jeopardize their friendship for a quick fling that would fizzle out and leave them both bitter.

"Wise, I guess." Duane seemed uncomfortable. "And look, I wanted to set something straight now. In case you're jumping to any wrong conclusions, I didn't kill my wife and her lover when I found out about them. I've heard the rumors that some people like to spread in this town but it's pretty hard to off someone for cheating when you don't yet know about it. The first thing I knew about her affair was when I came home and she'd packed her stuff and left me a note stuck to the fridge telling me she didn't love me, hadn't for a long time and was going away with a guy ten years younger than me.

"Don't get me wrong, I was furious, and I think if I could have got my hands on Curtis Lowell, I would have done some damage, but I wouldn't have hit Louisa no matter how mad she made me. The only time I ever hit a woman was when we had to drag Mary Beth off her husband's body after she'd stabbed him so many times, he was bleeding everywhere. She had another knife on her and went to stab me in the eye, of all places. I punched her in self-defense, but it was just the once and she went down like a sack of shit. I still feel kinda bad about it, but at least I still have both eyeballs which is more than can be said for poor Arlen when his wife had finished with him."

Maria couldn't help but believe him. He seemed genuinely remorseful about smacking Mary Beth. Her gut was telling her that Duane Holt was not a wife beating, daughter killing, murdering kind of man. But she would still have to do some digging to confirm it. Even the nicest people could kill if pushed too hard.

They reached the turn off for the long, overgrown drive to the hospital and all three of them fell silent.

Here we go again, Maria thought.

SEVEN

Maria stared out of the window. A low-lying ground mist snaked across the overgrown driveway. Her gut was tied in knots knowing that they were going back to check the tower.

"I wish they'd razed this place to the ground last year like they were supposed to." The chief shook his head. "I've never hated a building more."

At the wheel, Frankie frowned. "Why didn't they?"

"Some do-gooder from the historical society thought the place should be saved, opened as a museum, and put up a fight. They didn't win, but they slowed everything down. If I could get my damn hands on them." He stopped. "I wouldn't... I'm not...'

From the back seat, Maria patted his shoulder. "I would feel the same. If this place had been nothing but rubble, Riley wouldn't be missing."

"Easier to blame everyone else than yourself, isn't it?"

"You weren't to blame. You didn't know she had come here. I read the report. You were working a car wreck on the county line."

"I was—that damn Jim Smith drove himself right through

the gas station window. He was lucky he didn't decapitate himself, the drunken fool."

The drive opened up and the hospital loomed in front of them. The ground mist made it look like something straight out of a horror movie. Headlights shone from down the drive and yet Maria couldn't tear her gaze away from the tower and the black shape that was watching them out of the window. Her skin crawled and the hairs on the back of her neck bristled, as whatever it was stepped away from the open space. Maria blinked then squinted to see if her eyes were playing tricks on her, but she knew they weren't. Something dark was waiting for them up in that tower and it wasn't Riley Holt.

Duane and Frankie were already out of the car while she stayed transfixed by the tower. Her door opened and Frankie leaned in.

"What's up?"

She peered up into his eyes and she knew he could see the fear in them.

"Nothing, it was probably nothing."

He screwed his face up. "Nah, you look like you've seen a ghost."

"There's something up there. It's not good."

He hesitated. "Do we need a priest?"

"I don't know what we need but I don't think we can deal with it on our own. I wonder if Missy and Emilia would be willing to come take a look. I'd feel better with their input."

"You want to call your elderly ghostbusting neighbors to come fight the good fight?"

"No, but I'd like them to tell us what we're dealing with. I don't trust anyone else. They lived through what we did, only for a hell of a lot longer, and I know they've been doing a lot of research about this kind of thing ever since. We can trust them. We don't need to worry about them telling us a load of crap."

He nodded. "We could bring them down here tomorrow."

A wave of tiredness washed over Maria. She looked at the entrance to the hospital and shuddered. Was it possible? Was Riley stuck inside there, someplace they couldn't find her? "Don't you leave me alone in there, Frankie."

"I promise. Where would I be if you disappeared and left me alone? I'd never cope without you."

He smiled, that big, cheesy grin which showed his almost perfectly straight, white teeth and made his eyes crinkle.

"The same place I'd be without you, Conroy."

The moment was broken when Duane appeared walking shoulder to shoulder with a woman who Maria assumed was Sammi Jo. The groundskeeper had a New York Yankees baseball cap on and her waist length, black hair was an impressive sight. She slipped a hair band off her wrist and tied her hair into a tight bun.

"Evening. I'm going to give you both the lowdown on the few simple rules I have for entering the building and I'd appreciate it if you listened and followed my instructions." At this, Maria wondered where she'd been earlier. It would have been helpful to have her advice then. "I know the chief and his team have been all over the place looking for Riley, bless her soul. They probably didn't listen to my advice, but I'm assuming there was so many of them it didn't matter."

"Sammi Jo, come on now, you're going to scare these nice city cops."

"Good. I'm being serious, Duane. Now, I know you don't believe me but for my sake I want you to do what I tell you. We're going inside way past a time that I'm comfortable with. There are only four of us so do not, whatever happens inside there, split up and don't leave anyone alone. I mean this. I learned the hard way about this place when things happened that I couldn't even begin to get my head around. That's when I went to visit my Aunt Dolores who told me everything I needed to know. She worked here until the day the hospital closed its doors and she said that things had always happened that couldn't be explained. Time shifted, shadows walked the halls and the patients never left, even after they passed on."

"Why didn't you tell the cops this?" asked Frankie.

Sammi Jo gave him an incredulous look. "My Aunt Dolores did go to the cops. Nobody believed her."

"I still don't," replied the chief, hotly. "It's just a building, for God's sake. It's a dump, it's falling down and it's dangerous, but it's not some haunted mansion."

"Riley went in there and never came out, Duane. How do you explain that?" Sammi had her hands on her hips.

All four of them were silent. Duane bowed his head. "We better do as she says," he said eventually.

Sammi Jo unlocked the front door. As Duane opened it, a rush of icy air flew out. Maria felt it go right through her body, shuddering at the intrusion, and then it was gone. The entrance was so shrouded in darkness it was hard to see anything except what was directly in front of them. Duane pulled out a huge flashlight, and Sammi Jo did the same.

"Maria, do you want to stay close to me? Frankie, you stay close to Sammi Jo. We do not separate, we stay together."

That moment Maria's phone vibrated and she tugged it out of her pocket to see a message from Harrison.

Supper and cocktails at the Rainbow Room, thirty minutes? xx

What she would give to be in her apartment about to go out for cocktails right now.

Working late, sorry. Tomorrow? xx

She pressed send, but it didn't work. She'd no signal and had no idea how that message had come through. Was something taunting her?

Sammi Jo frowned. "If you need a signal, you'll have to go way back past the cars. It's patchy at best around here and once we go inside, it's damn near non-existent."

Maria shook her head. "It's okay. It's not important."

Duane stepped inside; Maria stayed close to him. Frankie and Sammi Jo followed behind. The place felt different from when they were here earlier. It hadn't exactly felt friendly then, but now it was downright menacing. Or was Maria letting her imagination run away from her again? No one spoke. Maria tried to imagine the group of teenagers wandering around here in the dark. They were either braver than she was, or foolish. How could they have thought it would be fun to come inside this place at night? How wrong they'd been.

"Should we call out for Riley?" whispered Duane, as they made their way to the stairs.

Sammi Jo shook her head. "Don't attract any more attention than we already are."

He accepted her instruction, and Maria wondered how hard this must be for him. If it were her kid, she'd be running around the place screaming.

Another reason against having kids, she thought. She'd never particularly liked them in the first place, but she'd seen so much horror in her career that she didn't think bringing new life into the world was the right thing to do. Plus, she loved her job more than anything and couldn't afford distractions—or at least she usually loved her job. Right now, she wished she'd never agreed to form the strange case review team, and judging by the way Frankie was almost glued to Sammi Jo in front of her, so did he.

As she climbed the stairs, she could sense the presences of *others*. She wasn't sure exactly who those others were, but she knew they were there. In the dusty darkness Maria swore she could almost make out the faintest of blurred outlines of people. Some rocked from side to side, others had their heads bowed. One looked as if they were bundled into a straitjacket. Was her imagination making all of this up—or was she truly seeing the shadows of lost souls?

Sammi Jo stopped so abruptly Frankie slammed into the back of her. She held up a hand to quieten them, though none of them had spoken for several minutes. Then Maria heard it—the heavy shuffling of feet on the floor above them. Exchanging a look with Duane, she knew he was about to yell out for Riley, so she did the only thing she could and clamped her hand across his mouth. This was no easy task because he was much taller than her and she had to stand on her tiptoes to reach.

They made the strangest sight. Four grown adults hovering at the top of the staircase on the first floor, terrified beyond belief. The footsteps continued, and Maria knew that it wasn't Riley on the floor above. The kid would be running around terrified, not shuffling about, and these footsteps sounded far too heavy for the girl. When the shuffling stopped, Sammi Jo continued down the hallway.

Frankie grabbed hold of her arm and pointed to the floor above, then whispered, "Should we go up there? Check it out."

Maria turned to face all three of them. "We came to check the tower. That's what we should do."

Duane nodded even though his face was a mask of fear in the beam from the flashlight.

Sammi Jo narrowed her eyes. "It knows we're here."

Maria had so many questions for the woman who had the enormous task of being the caretaker for this place, but they'd have to wait until they got outside.

They continued to the next set of stairs. The air up on the second floor was much colder. Sammi Jo shone her light around. There was nothing there, or at least nothing they could see with their eyes, but Maria wondered whether if they took photos, the thing that lurked up here would show up. She took out her phone and began to snap away, taking a succession of pictures to look at when they were somewhere brightly lit and far away from here.

As they passed the treatment room, Maria paused. She was certain a voice beside her ear had whispered, *Help me!*

Sammi Jo and Frankie were way ahead of them along the corridor. She signaled to Duane, who shone his flashlight into the room. There was no one inside, yet Maria couldn't shake the feeling there was somebody there, they just couldn't see them.

She whispered, "Riley?"

Duane stared at her in disbelief. "What are you doing?" he asked. "She's not in there."

Maria stepped inside. She could hear the words *Help me* being repeated inside her head.

"I want to help you," she replied to thin air. "Where are you?"

And then the whispers stopped. It was silent for a moment, and next thing Maria knew she was being dragged by her elbow out of the room and along the corridor by Duane, who seemed desperate to catch up to the others. She couldn't hear the voice now, but she was sure it had been Riley; it had sounded so young and afraid. They reached the others who stood by the small door to the tower. Frankie had one eyebrow raised, and Maria immediately pulled her arm away from Duane's.

Sammi Jo slid the two bolts back and looked at Duane. "You're ready for this?"

"No," he replied stiffly, "but it has to be done."

Maria watched as Sammi Jo inserted the rusted, old brass key into the lock. *We shouldn't be doing this,* she thought. *We're going to let it out—whatever it is...*

Maria wanted to run outside, get into the car and drive straight back to Manhattan. At this moment, she hated Frankie for bringing her here. She felt a burning rage inside her chest that came out of nowhere. She wanted to punch his lights out, punch the wall, punch anything really, the blackness inside her was so consuming. Then the door opened and Sammi Jo shone her flashlight into the dark void, illuminating a steep, narrow staircase full of cobwebs. It didn't look as if anyone had been up here in a very long time. It didn't look like the kind of place Riley would have wanted to explore on her own, even if she'd somehow found a key to get in here.

Sammi Jo turned to them. "Ready?"

Maria shook her head. She'd never be ready to see inside that tower, but she dutifully followed them. This time she was happy to be last because it meant she could be first out. Frankie, who was taller than Sammi Jo, brushed at the cobwebs with his arm, and they ascended the creaking, wooden stairs.

Maria whispered, "Why is it always the attic?"

Frankie shrugged but didn't answer. Everything was silent and still apart from the sound of their steps creaking under their weight, which would give them away if anyone was hiding up there. Sammi Jo was no longer in sight, and Maria felt her heart begin to race, but then Frankie took the next step and he, too, disappeared around the corner, followed by Duane and then Maria herself. The space they entered wasn't huge, but it was big enough that you could live comfortably up here—if for some reason you desired to live in the scariest building in New York State.

To her surprise, the tower was empty. Maria didn't know exactly what she'd expected to find up here, but it had been more than this. The disappointment on Duane's face was too much to bear. He looked devastated, and Maria realized how much he'd been hoping to find Riley in here, despite there being no way she could have gotten inside. She patted his back softly.

Frankie crossed the floor to the large window and looked down. "This is pretty high up. Is that why they never boarded it up?"

"They did board it up," replied Sammi Jo, "only it fell off. They boarded it again—that one fell off. We gave up after four attempts to board it up. So now we keep it locked, so no stupid kids come up here and fall out, breaking their necks." A look of horror crossed Sammi Jo's face. "Duane, I'm sorry..."

Duane held up his hand. "You're right, only stupid kids would be dumb enough to come in here at all. Let's get out of here, I've had enough for one night."

Maria had never wanted to hug a relative stranger so much in her life—and she was more of a high-five kind of gal than a hugger. Turning toward the stairs, she saw a black shadow move across the back wall from the corner of her eye and let out a screech. It was fast, and she had a feeling she wasn't supposed to see it. The shadow grew as it pulsated with darkness, then it rushed toward her, and Maria stumbled backwards. She could feel herself falling toward the gaping hole that had once been a window and realized that she'd rather fall out of it than let whatever that shadow thing was touch her. She let out another high-pitched scream of complete terror as the shadow creature came to within inches of her face and she could smell its fetid breath that stunk of rotting leaves, and then she felt nothing except a rush of cool night air as she tumbled back toward the empty window.

Maria heard Frankie yell as she fell in slow motion. Panicked thoughts raced through her head. What would happen if—when—she died from the fall? Would she be stuck here forever, too? Next thing she knew two strong arms were gripping her wrists and she was dragged back inside the tower and into Frankie's embrace.

"Jesus, Maria, you were nearly wiped out. Are you okay?" He had a tight hold of her, and she didn't push him away. Her teeth chattered and she felt a fear so primal that it turned her blood to ice water.

Duane looked out of the window, shining his flashlight down onto the covered porch over the entrance. Sammi Jo watched on in horror.

"We have to get out of here," Frankie said. "How the hell did she get pushed?"

Maria wasn't going to argue. Something had just tried to kill her, she was certain of it. She wanted to run and never come back, only she didn't think her legs would let her.

Duane nodded. "Let's go. My daughter is not in here."

Maria didn't say it, but she begged to differ. Riley Holt was in this hospital somewhere, just not where they could see her.

Maria soon found herself being led toward the stairs by Frankie, who didn't let go of her hand. Her feet felt sluggish, like she didn't want to leave, even though that's what she wanted more than anything in the world.

Once they were all out of the tower, Sammi Jo slammed the door shut, locked it then bolted it. They didn't speak as they followed her past the empty rooms and through the smell of mold and decay as they hurried to the ground floor. Finally, Frankie pulled her out through the porch into the wonderful fresh air.

Before he left, Duane paused in the entrance and shouted at the top of his voice: "Riley!"

There was no reply, although Maria was certain she heard a high-pitched giggle come from somewhere inside. He joined them outside and Sammi Jo slammed the door shut and locked it, before hurrying down the steps to get to her car. Frankie still held Maria's hand tightly. She was frozen to the core and his body heat made her feel a little better. He bundled her into the back of Duane's cruiser, took his jacket off to wrap around her shoulders, and climbed in next to her.

Putting an arm around her, Frankie pulled her close. "You're frozen, Maria, it must be the shock."

She couldn't speak, as if her voice was stuck inside her throat, and for that she was glad because she didn't think she would be coherent if she could find it. She heard Duane thank

Sammi Jo, who sped away. Duane got in the cruiser, turned the engine on and blasted the heat.

"Are you okay? My God, you almost—" He stopped himself. "I'll get you to my house and we can sort you out, or do you need to go to the hospital?"

Frankie answered for her. "She's fine, just shocked. Your house is good, anywhere is good as long as it's far away from this damn place."

Duane started the engine and Maria squeezed her eyes shut as she tried to block out the image of that black shadow, made from a thousand screaming souls, that had rushed toward her.

EIGHT

Duane's house was a red brick detached bungalow with a black metal fence running around the perimeter and a bright yellow front door. She still hadn't found her voice and wondered if she ever would again. *Or had that thing stolen it right before it tried to steal her soul?* Duane helped her out of the car, and she let him, wishing she didn't feel so damn useless. He led them both up the steps and into a brightly lit grey kitchen that was modern, and gorgeous—or it would have been if it had a splash of color to it.

Duane sat Maria down at the table, while Frankie hovered nearby looking unsure what to do with himself, until Duane said, "Take a seat, I'll get us a drink."

Maria assumed he meant beers: a cop's go-to liquid refreshment after coffee. Instead, he filled a kettle and got mugs and a teapot out of the cupboard. Duane Holt was full of surprises.

"Tea is good for shock. It will help you, Maria, especially if it's sweet. My mom is English and swears by a hot cup of tea for just about every situation there is."

Maria didn't have the heart to tell him she didn't drink tea after he'd gone to so much trouble. She watched as he poured out three mugs, added milk and passed one to her. She wrapped her numb fingers around it, still unable to speak.

"I don't know what to say, Maria. I saw you get pushed backwards toward that open window, but I saw nobody pushing you."

Frankie nodded. "One moment you were standing there, the next whoosh you were about to freefall out. What did you see? Or did it happen too quickly? And don't tell me you tripped because you clearly didn't."

She sipped the hot liquid, not really tasting it, just hoping that it was enough to thaw her vocal cords. Could you get struck dumb with fear? She managed a small cough.

"I saw a black shape on the wall..." Her voice was barely a whisper, but she felt a sense of relief that she still had one.

Frankie leaned toward her. "What kind of shape?"

"I don't know. It was like a round thing, a mass of some sort. It grew and grew until it left the wall and was rushing toward me." She closed her eyes, trying to block out the image and the memory of that dreadful smell. Was this what Riley had seen before she disappeared?

"Did it push you?" Duane asked. "You flew backwards like someone had shoved you in the chest, hard."

"I don't know. Did I not just trip backwards in fear?"

Duane's blue eyes watched her face intently and she got the feeling he was trying to figure out if she was telling the truth.

Frankie sighed. "No, you did not."

Maria took another sip of the tea. "It was dark, and it felt evil. To be honest, it scared the shit out of me. I know that it wanted me to die because—"

She stopped herself. How could she know what that thing had wanted? She wasn't a psychic. And yet she swore she had seen the trapped souls of the patients who couldn't escape the building. She knew that whatever it was had wanted to add her soul to its collection, and that it had most likely already taken Riley's. But how could she put that into words?

"Maybe we scared it by going into its lair. It's pretty obvious that's where it hides itself away. We are messing with things we don't understand. Duane, I have two dear friends who live next door to me. They are elderly, but they are excellent at figuring this stuff out. Would you mind if I called them to come help?"

"You mean they're psychics?"

"I guess you could call them that, but they are not kooks. They helped us deal with something as equally terrifying during the last case we worked. And they've spent years researching this kind of thing."

Duane got to his feet and paced up and down the kitchen. Finally, he turned to look at her.

"Okay. I can't deny that what I saw inside that hospital was unexplainable. But none of this is public knowledge. I don't want the press to get hold of it, me calling some psychics in to help. They'll think I'm losing my mind."

"I'll speak to them. They don't talk to the press or anyone really about what they do. They are very private people."

He stopped pacing and turned to look at them both. "I don't know what to do. My mom is in England visiting her sick sister. I can't get hold of Louisa to tell her our daughter is missing, and I feel as if I've been sucked into some weird Tim Burton film and I'm waiting for Michael Keaton to tell me to call for Beetlejuice or something."

Frankie took charge. "We can't do anything now. It's late. I think we should get ourselves back to the city. Maria can have a hot shower, speak to her neighbors and get some sleep. We'll be back here tomorrow. We need to speak to Riley's other friends and check out the cemetery. Did you know there was one on the land?"

Duane nodded. "We had the dogs out searching and nothing."

"Well, tomorrow in the daylight we'd like to take a proper look around the grounds. Is that okay with you, chief?"

"Of course, anything you want."

Frankie stood up and motioned for Maria to do the same. She wanted nothing more than to get back to her apartment. "We may be able to trace your wife," Frankie said. "I have some contacts who are pretty good at finding people who don't want to be found."

"I'd appreciate that. As mad as I am with her for disappearing without a trace, she's still Riley's mom and she needs to know."

Maria managed to smile. "Of course, she does. Maybe you should get some rest, too. Sleep in your own bed, have a hot shower and something to eat. Dorothy said you haven't been home much. We have a lot to do tomorrow, and you'll feel much better if you get some rest."

He looked offended but he didn't argue with her. "Thank you. I'm sorry you got hurt."

"I'm a big girl. I've had a lot worse over the years, but thank you, Duane."

Duane dropped them off at their car. Maria wondered if he would go inside afterwards, but he didn't. He waved at them, did a U-turn, then drove back in the direction he'd come from.

"He seems like a nice guy who is having the worst time."

Frankie opened the car. "Yeah, I get that it's tough when you lose your wife to another guy. Hell, you know that I've been there, and I hit rock bottom for a while, but you kept me going. It's a shame he doesn't have his own Maria."

"They should clone me for all those cops who need a personal support system. I'd never have to work another damn day, just spend all my time drinking cocktails and not worrying about having my soul sucked out of my body by some stinking black shadow thing."

"Hey, you're mine; I get all of you."

"*Hey*, you sound like some perverted stalker. I'm not yours. I belong to me."

"Suit yourself, but you know damn well you couldn't live without me in your life."

Maria rolled her eyes. "Jeez, you're more deluded than I thought."

She didn't argue with him though because it was true; he was her best friend, and she wouldn't trade him for anything.

DECEMBER 1960

Faye soaked in the bath until the water from the faucet ran cold. She dried herself on the rough towels, the kind she was used to from her younger days. Her mom used to tell her it was good for the skin, and she guessed it kind of was. She had no moisturizer to smooth over herself like she usually would, and she had to wash her hair with some cheap, nasty shampoo, but she sure did feel better. Dolores had been right: a hot bath had made her feel a little more like herself. Her overnight case had been opened and was on the bed, so she dressed in a pair of cut-off black slacks and a black polo-neck. Despite the radiator being on, it was still chilly in the hospital.

Wandering across to the window, which even up here had metal bars across it so no one could jump out, she stared down at the grounds. They were pretty. Someone worked hard to keep them looking so nice. A young man in a red and white checked shirt with a wheelbarrow full of tools stopped on the lawn, as if he'd noticed her watching, and looked up. She waved, and he waved back, then he did a little bow which made her giggle. He couldn't know who she was from this distance, not with wet hair, but he'd made her smile. Some folks were just nice to everyone and that was what mattered in this world. She'd had to learn the hard way that Hollywood was not full of nice people. Sure, they made her famous and turned her into a glamorous movie star, but they weren't nice about it. The groundsman waved at her once more then pushed the wheelbarrow across the lawn and into the wooded area behind.

There was no hairdryer that she could find so she toweldried her hair. Her makeup and beauty products had been taken out of her bag but there was still a jar of Pond's cold cream, so she smoothed some over her skin, giving it a good lathering to make sure it kept its youthful appearance. Sitting down on the edge of the single bed, she sighed. When had she become this obsessed with her appearance and not aging? Her friend had told her about a cosmetic surgeon who could keep her looking this way forever, but she wasn't too sure she wanted to go that far.

"Look at you, Miss Miller. You look all kinds of fresh now. Would you like me to blow dry your hair? Now, I'm not saying I can do what your usual stylist can but I have a hairdryer so we can give it a shot."

Faye grinned at Dolores. "You are a sweetheart and I'm quite happy for you to do whatever you please. It takes a lifetime to get it curled and primped into its usual shape."

Dolores closed the door behind her. "I hope you're feeling a little better now you're not locked up like some caged animal. I don't know why they did that to you, and I'd be speaking to your doctor about it. If you find out that they ordered it, then I think you need to find yourself a better doctor. Forgive me for speaking out of turn. I just don't think that this is the right place for you, and I don't know why they thought it was."

Faye nodded. "I don't know either. If I write a letter, could you post it out for me, Dolores? Joe, my ex-husband, would be furious if he knew I was locked in here against my will."

"Honey, you write that letter, and I will post it on my way

home. I wouldn't trust the post here to get it sent out. I'll come see you before I finish and get it from you. Make sure you write it, won't you? Otherwise, you could be stuck in here for a lot longer than you could ever need to be."

Faye smiled at the woman. She wasn't much older than she was yet seemed to know an awful lot about everything.

Once Dolores had fetched the hairdryer, Faye sat on the edge of the bed so she could dry her hair. A part of her thought she shouldn't be wasting her time, but another welcomed the care and the touch of the nurse's soft hands as they parted then brushed her hair. She'd never wanted to end up sad and lonely, with a heart broken into so many tiny pieces. Too many people wanted to know her for who she wasn't, and when they saw the real her, they got scared and walked out of her life, leaving her alone. She could count the number of friends she had on one hand. Dolores, she thought, would make a wonderful friend. She was kind, caring and straight talking.

When the hairdryer was turned off, she felt sad that it was done. She could have sat this way all day, but she was being selfish and keeping Dolores from her other patients.

"There you go, Miss Miller. It's not perfect."

Faye stood up and looked in the tiny mirror on the wall. "It's wonderful—you are a natural at hairdressing. Thank you for everything. How can I ever repay you?"

Dolores smiled and shook her head. "All I need from you is for you to try and get that poor girl next door to speak so we can get her out of here, if that's still okay with you. I have to go watch over the treatments this afternoon. I'd rather not but if I'm not there, someone who doesn't care about the patients will be, and that's not good for them. Remember you're paying to be here, don't put up with no crap from anyone."

Faye stood up and gave Dolores the briefest of hugs. She wasn't sure if patients were allowed to hug nurses, but she didn't care and she saw the woman's eyes begin to fill up.

"Well, if I ever thought that I'd see the day I'd be on hugging terms with you, Miss Miller."

"Faye, please, although you could call me by my real name if you want."

"Marilyn?"

She laughed. "Lord no, she's like a blood-sucking conjoined twin. Norma is just fine; I only have a couple of people who still call me that."

"I would love to, Norma, but I might get myself in trouble. We best stick with Miss Miller or Faye if no one else is around. I hope that's okay with you, and you can understand that."

"Faye is just fine then; I don't want to get you into any bother, not when you've been so kind to me, especially when I was so desperate for a little kindness."

Dolores smiled at her and nodded, then turned to leave. Faye stared in the mirror and whispered, *Will the real woman please come forward? I don't know who I am anymore and I'm tired of this.*

Up here was so quiet compared to downstairs. She walked out of her room into the hallway and looked around. The woman she'd seen earlier with the small suitcase was being shown into a room a little further down. Faye knocked on her neighbor's door softly then pushed it open a little to see a teenage girl sitting on the bed, her knees pulled up to her chest, her arms hugging them close to her.

"Hello, I'm Faye. I'm in the room next door and I'm awfully bored. Can I come sit with you for a little while?"

The girl stared at her with a look of mild confusion etched across her face. She looked wild, terrified like a scared rabbit, and it broke Faye's heart. She stepped inside, not sure if the girl might attack her, but she'd promised Dolores that she'd give it a go. Walking to the window, she looked down on the gardens.

"It looks so lovely out there, doesn't it? I wish I could go for a walk in the fresh air. How about you, would you like to do that? We could go together if you don't want to go on your own."

The girl only stared at her, and so she carried on talking.

"I was put here in one of the padded rooms downstairs, you know. I woke up here and didn't even remember coming here or why. It scared me so bad, and I cried a lot, then I realized my shrink must have sent me here. She is for the chop when I get out. Is that what happened to you?"

The girl watched her intently, and then shook her head.

"How did you end up in the nuthouse, then? Did you do something bad?"

This time she shook her head even faster. "I don't know how I got here..." Her voice was barely a whisper, but at least she'd spoken. Faye smiled to encourage her. "What year is it? Everyone is wearing old-fashioned clothes and the nurses' uniforms... I've seen pictures from the olden days and that's what they wore."

"The olden days? What do you mean, like back in the nineteen-thirties?"

The girl's face screwed up into a mask of confusion. "No, what year is it now?"

"It's December nineteen-sixty. I can't tell you what day because I don't know that."

Her eyes widened and she stared at Faye, panicked. Her breathing was fast.

"How? I don't understand how this is December nineteen-sixty. This place... it looks familiar but not how I know it."

"You mean you had some kind of breakdown and your mind's gone blank, like in a movie? Or maybe you've got a head full of ghosts?"

"No, I don't think I have... I feel so weird, as if everything is a dream. Am I dreaming or are you real? Are you sure you're called Faye? You look an awful lot like a famous movie star?"

She smiled at the girl who seemed to be having no trouble

talking now. "So many questions for someone who has no idea who they are or where they came from. I'm Faye whilst I'm here. What's your name?"

"I'm not sure, everything seems a bit fuzzy."

"Well, mystery girl, Dolores, the kind nurse, is worried about you. She doesn't think you belong here, although neither do I if I'm honest. Maybe we can figure out what you're called and where you're from." Faye looked down at the girl's bare feet. "Maybe you're from the future? Is that why you only have one shoe? Did it get lost in a time machine?"

She laughed and at the same time watched the girl for signs that she might be completely delusional, but she didn't come across as someone who was like that. She sounded scared and bewildered.

"I don't know where my shoe is. I don't have a time machine, I don't think. I think I was dragged by something and hit my head. Then I was dragged here."

Faye thought the poor kid must have hit her head a lot harder than she'd realized by the way she was talking.

The girl sat up straight, fear turning her face a ghostly shade of white.

"Who dragged you here?"

"Oh God, I don't know, but it was horrible." She began to cry, big loud sobs that filled the room and Faye felt terrible that she'd upset her. She crossed the room and sat next to her on the bed.

"I don't know what you're talking about, but if I was you, I wouldn't say any of that to the nurses except for Dolores, because you're talking like you are crazy and they are never going to let you leave if you do that. You don't want to be stuck here forever, kid, it's not a good place."

The girl looked at her. "Why are you here?"

Faye laughed. "I'm here because I created a monster that takes over my whole life and drives everyone who I ever like and love away. I drink too much champagne and pop too many pills but I'm also here because my husband is having an affair and I think I lost it when I found out. The details are a little hazy because of the state I was in."

"I'm sorry, that's so sad. My mom left, too."

"I'm sorry to hear that. Maybe that's why you're here. Did you have a breakdown when she left you?"

"No, I was angry with her for doing that to my dad, but it didn't send me insane." She looked at Faye. "Sorry, I didn't mean you are insane."

"That's okay, between you and me I probably am. I'm also a deep kind of sad, which hurts my heart, but I suppose I shouldn't let a man, or anyone, make me feel that way. Have you got a boyfriend?"

"No, I have friends who are boys but no boyfriend."

Faye could tell the girl was studying her intently, but she didn't find it awkward like she normally did. She didn't know the kid and yet she felt sorry for her. She must be really delusional if she thought someone had dragged her here. She would tell Dolores what she'd said. The poor girl must need help if she thought that.

"Well, whatever you do, make sure you don't rely on a man to make you happy. You have to make your own happiness in this world. I've been married three times and I'm only just starting to learn that."

"I wouldn't do that. Where I'm from, girls and women are all very into self-care, empowerment, being successful on their own without a guy kind of thing. It's a whole vibe and Instagram is full of it."

Faye let out a small giggle. "You do say some funny things. What is Instagram?"

"Where I'm from we have these smartphones we carry everywhere with us. We can video call, go on the internet and do just about everything with them."

"Internet, what's that?"

Riley smiled at her. "I really am in nineteen-sixty, aren't I?"

Faye nodded at her slowly, then smiled. "Say, hey, can you take me to the future with you? You could show me the internet."

"I wish that I could, but I don't know how to get back there, and I don't know if you would still be the same age when you got there."

"How old are you in the future?"

"The same."

"Then I would be the same. I'm thirty-four now. That would be so much fun. I could start again, and no one would know who I am."

A look of sadness washed over the girl's face and she didn't speak.

"Why do you look so sad?"

"Everybody knows who you are. I mean, like, the whole world, and everyone loves you so much. You're this huge icon; there are posters, coffee cups, dolls, books, so many books about you and they even keep making Netflix documentaries about you."

"They do?"

"You're more famous in the future than you are now."

"I am, huh? How strange, I wonder why. I'm not that good at acting. I mean, I love it and I used to enjoy it but now it's such a chore—I find everything a total chore. What's *Net fix*?"

"Netflix; it's a station that has lots of films on it you watch straight from the TV instead of going to the movies."

"Well, how about that. I think I'd still like to go to your future. It would be better than what I have now. I could be my own person, maybe let my hair go back to being brown, grow it long so nobody knew who I was."

The girl smiled at her. "You'd still be you and beautiful. I would love you to come back with me. I'd show you how to work a smartphone and we could watch movies together; it would be so cool."

"I think it would be cool, too—we could be girlfriends and just have fun."

The door opened and a nurse stood staring at them both.

"Faye, the doctor would like to see you now, if you follow me, please."

Faye smiled at the girl. "We could hide from head shrinks, too." Then she winked at her.

She followed the nurse out and turned to look back at the girl who was now staring out of the window. What a strange creature. Imagine believing you're a time traveler. She guessed if it made the girl feel better about her situation, who was she to ruin that for her? Going to the future could be so much fun, if only it were real. She could escape this awful life she'd created for herself in her own time.

NINE

Maria had never been so glad to get out of a place as she had Beacon Hill. It was the kind of small town she'd thought she might move to when she finally got fed up with city life, to live in a house like Abraham's with a garden to tend to and not much stress. Now, though, she'd seen a side to the place that most people wouldn't know existed and she was glad to be out of there.

"Are you really okay? That was pretty damn scary."

"Honestly, Frankie, I don't know. Thank you for saving my ass again."

He laughed. "Your ass is mine to save. I wouldn't do any of this without you, you know that."

"Still. I thought that thing was going to kill me and steal my soul. Do you think that's what it does? Because I do. I think that's why that building is full of patients who died and can't escape. That's a horrible thought."

"I think we should get you home, maybe call at the Cat for a beer to help you sleep, and then we can have a serious think in the morning about our options."

She smiled, knowing that he was telling her to leave the case behind for tonight. He was scared and wouldn't admit it. The guy who had binge-watched every ghost-hunting series on cable TV wasn't as brave as he thought. Maria didn't push it. She also wanted to forget the incident had ever happened, but she knew that it would be forever stuck in her head. How did people live with this stuff? How had Lorraine and Ed Warren dealt with all the scary crap they faced then gone home to their family and acted normal? Maybe Maria needed to start reading up about them. It might help her with these cases. *God damn it.* That ten-thousand-dollar sweetener for dealing with this weird shit wasn't worth a single cent.

Maria jumped out of Frankie's car onto the sidewalk in front of her apartment building.

"You want me to come and tuck you in to bed?" He winked at her, and she almost said yes because she didn't want to be alone with her thoughts. Instead, she waved one hand at him.

"I'm a tough broad, like you keep telling me. I don't need a man to tuck me in."

"What about the rich guy? Bet you'd let him do it?"

"The rich guy lives across town, and no, I want to be on my own tonight and process what the hell happened to me."

She slammed the car door and waved him away. Then she went inside her apartment block and into the lift to her floor. As she walked past Missy's door she wondered if it was too late to knock, checking her watch. Better to catch her now, she thought, in case she disappeared somewhere in the morning. It made her heart happy seeing Missy and Emilia living together after all the wasted years they spent apart. She knocked on the door and heard the familiar shuffling of Missy in the too-big soft shoes she wore indoors, then her voice came, muffled, through the door.

"Maria, is that you knocking so late?"

"It is, sorry to disturb you both."

The door opened and there was Missy in a pair of silk PJ's

in a striking shade of emerald green that made her grey hair sparkle in the dim light.

"Come in, Maria, and tell me what's bothering you."

Maria followed her inside hoping she wasn't disturbing the two nicest women she'd had the pleasure of ever meeting. They'd become more than friends once they'd realized how deep their love for each other was and Maria thought it was the purest, sweetest thing she'd ever known. It also gave her hope that one day in the future she might find someone she loved as deeply as they loved one another. It was proof that love had no time limit and could happen when you least expected it.

Emilia was taking a wine glass from the cupboard in the open-plan kitchen. She waved it in the air and Maria, despite not being a big wine drinker, nodded. She was going to need something to help her get to sleep tonight.

Missy glanced at Emilia then back at Maria. "Honey, do you want to tell us what's wrong? Is that big brute Frankie okay? Have you dumped Harrison?"

Emilia passed her a glass of red wine and Maria took a sip, trying not to grimace but glad of the warmth. Her insides hadn't really thawed out since she'd left the hospital.

"No, Harrison is not dumped. You have to be in a relationship to dump someone, and Frankie is fine. We went to a job in Beacon this afternoon."

"Beacon is a long way from the city. Why?"

"Frankie has an old friend in the PD there, and he asked for his help."

Missy nodded. "Loyal, I'll give him that much. Carry on."

"A teenager went into an abandoned mental asylum and never came out. Her three friends did and all of them saw a black shadow, and they think it took her. But it's not just that. As I walked around, I could sense the patients who had died. They were still there, lots of them watching us."

Emilia stared at her, while Missy did the talking.

"So, you've been there and had a look for yourself. You think the kids are telling the truth? There's more to it, isn't there? You saw something and now you're scared to go back. Are wondering if you are losing your mind? Questioning whether something that can take souls and trap them in that place really exists?"

Maria took another large sip of wine and nodded. "You're good."

"It comes with age. Now, what are we going to do about that?"

"You're both doing nothing, and staying here where you're safe, but I'd appreciate some advice about what I should do."

Emilia smiled at her. "I haven't visited Beacon in forever. I hear they have a dessert shop that's to die for. I'm in for a road trip."

Missy stared at Emilia with pure love in her eyes and Maria took the moment and savored it. She hoped she'd look at someone the same way at some point in her life.

"That's not what I'm asking you to do. I was going to, but then as I got back to the city, I realized it was too dangerous. I'm not putting either of you in harm's way. As I say, advice would be great if you can give me any."

"I kinda think we need to go get a feel of the place first, Maria. It's hard to assess something from here. And besides, I'm bored, bored, bored beyond belief, and I know Emilia is, too. We were only just saying we could do with getting out of the Village for a few hours."

"It's far too dangerous..."

"For what? A couple of old broads who have nothing better to do with their time?"

"What happened to you tonight, Maria?" Missy asked. "Your face is paler than Emilia's and she hasn't let her skin see the sun since nineteen fifty-two."

Maria almost spat a mouthful of wine over herself and choked on it instead, resulting in a coughing fit.

Emilia slapped her back and rubbed it. "Take no notice of Miss Smarty Pants. I'm just particular about not getting it all wrinkled."

It was Missy's turn to laugh. "Lord, you are so funny. Those Botox injections have nothing to do with that, do they? Considering the fact that we are both in our eighties."

"Well, we can't all be blessed with good genes like you, Missy."

"Everyone knows Black don't crack, white girl."

The pair of them doubled over laughing and Maria joined in. Her mother was Latino and she hoped she'd inherited her good genes. The warmth and love she felt for the two senior women, giggling like a pair of teenage girls, filled her heart.

"Honestly, any advice is good."

"Honey, we have no advice. We've done our research, but we didn't exactly go to school for dealing with evil entities. We got sucked into the first one under duress and over the years have kind of fallen into the whole communicating with spirits sort of thing. If we can help you to find that girl or her body, God rest her soul, then it's got to be done. Either of us could get summoned off by the good man himself at any time. Life is precious, but who are we to ignore someone who needs help that we might be able to give?"

"You're both so kind." She sighed. "The hospital has a tower. When we were up there, a black shadow rushed toward me and shoved me out of an open window. Frankie just managed to grab hold of me in time or else I'd have been smashed to pieces when I hit the ground below."

Both women gasped and Missy grabbed her hand. "Girl, you really need to be more careful. If it has that kind of power, then it's way over yours and Frankie's heads. It might be way over ours, too, but unless we can get a feel of the place then we won't know. When are you going back?"

"First thing. There's an old cemetery in the grounds we want to search."

"How early is first thing?"

"Frankie is picking me up around seven thirty, but he's always late so nearer to eight am."

Emilia laughed. "Missy hasn't seen seven thirty am since I moved in here, but me, I'm up early. I always have been an early riser, so I'll make sure we're ready. Frankie won't mind a couple of ride alongs, will he?"

Maria grinned at her. "Not when it's you two. You're his favorite broads—after me, of course." She finished the wine and stood up.

Missy watched her. "Why don't the pair of you just get together? It would make both your lives so much easier if you lived together, and I bet he's great in the sack. Plus, he's nice to look at. He missed his calling. He could have been an actor with those rugged good looks."

Maria's mouth dropped open. "I... we're best friends and I love him dearly. If we became more than that and it didn't work, I'd be losing my most treasured friend and the best work partner I could ever wish for."

Missy shrugged. "True, but what if it did work, have you considered that?"

Emilia shook her head. "Missy, she's got Harrison."

"No, she hasn't. She won't commit to him either, and I know it's because you find his money intimidating but darling, money doesn't mean a thing except that you can pay your utilities and buy groceries without having to worry. Money can never buy you happiness. Not the deep-down happiness you find by having someone in your life that you can share the good, the bad and downright ugly times with. Trust me, I spent so many years pining for Emilia that I wasted most of my life, and the money I earned didn't make a difference."

Maria didn't know what to say, so she smiled and kissed them both on the cheek. "Good night. If you're not up in time, don't worry about it."

Then she walked out of the apartment and into her own next door, wondering if she was that transparent or whether Missy was just that good a judge of character. Whatever it was, she always seemed to know Maria better than anyone. But she wouldn't get involved with Frankie no matter how good he looked—or smelled—because she valued his friendship far more than a quick roll in the sack.

Sliding the deadbolts across the door, Maria switched the lights on and began her nightly check of every space a person could hide in. There weren't many, but she didn't think she could ever take her safety for granted, not after what happened a few months ago. Every closet and room checked, she finally relaxed, took a hot shower and did some light reading before bed. Then she turned off the light and closed her eyes; she'd an early start and didn't want to waste any of her beauty sleep or brain power because she needed every bit to help find Riley Holt and bring her home safe.

TEN

The next morning, Maria was woken by knocking on her apartment door. She lay in bed wondering how she could have missed her alarm and blamed it on the large glass of wine. It wasn't a hangover that made her groan as she got herself up—not from only the one glass. It was the thought of having to now rush to get dressed while Frankie paced up and down outside her apartment. She quickly got into her black trousers, black roll-neck and black boots and rushed to open the door.

"Yeah, yeah, give me a minute, will you?"

Having unbolted the door, she blinked in surprise at the two women staring back at her.

"We thought you might try to sneak off without us. Good job you didn't, Maria. We spent an hour packing our cases. At our age you never know if you're going to need a heart zapper, pills or a hot water bottle."

Maria opened the door. "Come in. I'm not quite ready yet. I thought you were Frankie the way you were pounding on that door."

Missy and Emilia did as they were told, wheeling their carry-on cases behind them, and took a seat on her sofa.

"Won't be long," Maria told them, heading to the bathroom.

Maria ran the toothbrush over her teeth and rinsed with mouthwash. There wasn't time to do anything other than tie her hair in a high ponytail, rub tinted moisturizer across her face and apply a little eyebrow gel to smooth down her eyebrows, which could get wild when they needed waxing. The small diamond studs she put on sparkled in the light. They had been a gift from Harrison, and she wore them for work, and, well, for everything. She was too afraid to ask him how much they cost as she'd likely never wear them again. They'd end up locked in her gun safe for the rest of her life.

Spritzing herself with her favorite Jean Paul Gaultier So Scandal perfume, a gift from Frankie for her birthday, she grabbed her gun and badge from the locked safe in her closet, then wandered back to the lounge, where her neighbors were making themselves at home. Her phone vibrated, and she pulled it out of her pocket.

"Yeah," she said to Frankie, "we're ready to go, are you?"

"Outside in thirty seconds."

She hung up. Her stomach growled, so she grabbed a box of cereal bars from the kitchen cupboard and offered them around. Emilia looked horrified.

"You are not going out to do a full day's work on *that*, are you?"

Maria shrugged. "I overslept. If we have time, then Frankie will take us to Sam's to get a bagel and coffee but don't get your hopes up, ladies, because he's a pain in the ass when he's got to be some place. Actually, he's a pain in the ass most of the time."

Missy laughed. "That may be, but he's a handsome pain in the ass, I'll give him that."

"You haven't seen him lately. He's got some kind of beard going on. Next thing we know he'll be growing out his hair and wearing a man bun."

"Well, I do believe this trip is getting more exciting by the minute."

Maria tilted her head as she stared at Missy. What was with their sudden obsession with Frankie?

"Honey, just because we love each other dearly and are in a committed relationship it doesn't mean that we can't appreciate a good-looking man when we see one."

Emilia laughed. "Oh boy, she's a sucker for a handsome man. She just doesn't want to sleep with them; nothing wrong with looking though."

Maria laughed. "I'll be damned, you two are even funnier than I knew."

Hearing a running engine, Maria peered out of the window and saw Frankie's car waiting by the curbside.

"Time to go, ladies."

"Are you not stopping over?" asked Missy. "Make your life easier if you don't have to drive there and back every day."

Maria hadn't really thought about it, not wanting to spend a second longer in Beacon than was absolutely necessary.

"Can you ladies go tell Frankie I'll be down in a few moments, please?"

They headed for the elevator and Maria rushed into the bedroom to grab an overnight bag. She threw underwear, a change of clothes and a hairbrush into the travel bag she kept full of essential toiletries for emergencies. Then she pulled on her thick winter jacket and ran out the door. Missy and Emilia were laughing loudly by the time she got to the car and threw her bag in the trunk next to their cases and Frankie's overnight bag. Everybody had been ready for this except for her. It was like some kind of high school trip, only she was thirty-five and the youngest by several years.

She got into the passenger seat and fastened her safety belt. "I never got the memo."

Frankie looked sideways at her. "What memo?"

"The *pack a bag* one."

"The golden girls didn't get a memo and they're not complaining, are you, ladies?"

"Nope," Missy said with a laugh. "We're ready for some goddamn excitement and the company of a handsome guy."

Maria groaned. "Don't feed his ego, Missy. His head is big enough."

Frankie glanced at her. "What... you don't think I'm good looking?"

"I think you should get driving. We have a busy day."

He turned around and winked at Missy. "She won't admit it because she loves me too much."

Missy nodded but didn't answer him.

"Is anyone hungry?" Frankie asked as he pulled out.

Emilia shouted. "Famished, and I need coffee."

He winked at Maria. "Sam's it is then."

At Sam's, he double-parked so Maria could run in.

"Ladies," she said, turning to the backseat, "what would you like?"

Emilia shook her head. "Two lattes would be enough for us, not huge ones though or we'll need to pee every ten minutes. We ate before we came to yours, sugar. Make sure you get something satisfying, Maria."

Maria smiled. Those two were far savvier than she gave them credit for. She went inside to see Sam who blew her a kiss.

"Usual, Maria?"

She gave him a thumbs up. "Four lattes today, please." She smiled at the purple-haired girl working the coffee machine who shrugged and turned around to make the drinks without speaking a word.

"She's a real people person, ain't she?"

Marge, the waitress who had been working here since the

day it opened, rolled her eyes at the girl and Maria felt bad for her.

"It's okay. She can take a bit of criticism off her old granny."

Maria stared at her. "You have a granddaughter?"

"I have three to be exact. Saffy here decided to run away from home to come see me and work in the big city. I'm not complaining. I'm tired of being on my own. It's sure nice to have some company even if her conversation skills leave a lot to be desired."

Saffy turned her head and smiled at Marge. Her whole face lit up and Maria thought that underneath all that purple hair and heavy makeup was a pretty young woman waiting to be set free. When she passed the drinks tray over, Maria made a point of using her name.

"Thank you, Saffy, I'm Maria. Nice to meet you."

Sam came around the counter with her and Frankie's bagels. "Are you extra thirsty today or what?"

"I have company. It's a long story but I'll fill you in another day. Thanks, Sam."

She pushed two twenties toward Saffy, and Sam pushed them right back.

"This here woman is a real-life hero, Saffy. We don't ever take payment from her. It's the least we can do for everything she does out on those streets with no care about herself and her own safety. Her money is no good in here. And besides, someone has to make sure she eats. It makes me feel better knowing I'm that person. It's my way of giving something back."

He smiled at her and went back to the grill. Maria slid the money across to Saffy.

"Please take it. He's never going to be able to retire at this rate."

Saffy nodded, smiled back and slipped the money into the cash register before Sam noticed. Maria winked at her.

ELEVEN

Maria offered to drive, and Frankie declined, which suited her just fine. He hated it when she drove; he was a nervous passenger. This time she was happy to stare out the window as they passed through the Fahnestock State Park with a gorgeous lake and campsite plus acres of forest trails. It was a beautiful place to spend a day wandering. Maybe she should take Harrison there next time they went on a date, she thought. He did his best to come up with new inexpensive places they could visit, which must have given him quite the challenge, but it was the price he had to pay to spend time with her.

Missy and Emilia chattered away to Frankie. Maria smiled, enjoying their company. She hoped she hadn't dragged them into something too dangerous. She would do her best to keep them safe.

Frankie turned onto Craig House Lane and Maria called the chief to see if he was already there. His cell rang out, but as Frankie rounded the bend and the gates to the old hospital came into view, so did his huge pickup.

"I guess he had an early start." Maria pulled the visor down and looked at the two women behind her. She could see Missy had one hand clamped on Emilia's arm as they peered out at the hospital for the first time.

"Wow," Missy muttered.

"Wow, indeed," whispered Emilia.

Frankie glanced nervously across at Maria, and she shrugged. They had insisted on coming and now she wished with all her heart that they hadn't. Frankie parked up as the chief climbed out of his pickup. He was dressed in a checked shirt and faded Levi's with a baseball cap pulled tight on his head that read *Beacon PD*. Frankie jumped out the car to open the door for Missy who stepped out onto the gravel. Maria did the same for Emilia, who nodded thank you to her.

Maria approached the chief and smiled. "Chief Holt, I'd like you to meet my two dear friends, Missy and Emilia."

He stepped toward them, taking hold of their small hands in his huge one and shook them warmly.

"I'm Duane, and I'm mighty pleased to meet you. I can't thank you enough for coming out here to take a look."

Missy lifted a finger to his cheek and stroked it tenderly. "We'll find your girl, Duane. I know that we will, and I'm sorry that you're going through this. No one should have to experience this kind of heartbreak."

He blinked furiously and for a moment Maria thought he was going to start bawling. She wouldn't have blamed him one little bit. If this was her child, she didn't think she'd be able to string two words together, never mind carry on working and looking for her.

He smiled at Missy. "Thank you, I appreciate that."

"I know you do, honey. Now, let's not waste time."

Missy walked toward the front of the hospital. Her eyes were immediately drawn up to the tower, then her entire body shuddered from her head down to her feet. "Oh dear."

Maria rushed to her side, touching her arm to let her know

she would not let any harm come to her. Missy looked from the tower to the boarded-up windows of the hospital.

"So many souls trapped in this place. They shouldn't be here. They should have moved on a long time ago."

"Why are they here?" Maria asked. "You can sense them when you walk through the place. It's like there are hundreds of invisible eyes following your every move."

"They're trapped, honey, they can't move on because he won't let them."

A chilling blast of iciness made Maria's skin tingle with fear. "Who won't?"

"I'm not sure exactly just yet. He could be a couple of things but whichever it is, he's a collector of souls. It's shielding itself but it knows I'm here. You know it hides out in that tower, right?"

Maria nodded. "I do, after yesterday."

Missy walked toward the front doors, with Maria by her side and the others a few paces behind. At the door she pressed the palm of her hand against the board and closed her eyes for a few seconds. Then they snapped open.

"I need to go inside."

Maria shook her head. "I don't think it's a good idea. Can you not just do your stuff from outside?"

"I'm a big girl and stronger than I look. But I don't want Emilia anywhere near this place. Chief, would you be so kind as to take care of her for me and wait out here?"

Emilia shook her head. "No way, gal. If you go in, so do I, that was the deal. I'm not sitting out here while you're in there, no matter what is waiting inside."

Arms crossed, Missy looked at Maria. "Can you cuff her or something?"

"No cuffs, sorry," Maria replied. "How about you both do your thing from out here to keep me happy?"

Missy sighed. "Honey, there are some things you have to

face in life whether you want to or not—and this is one of them. So, are we going inside, then, or wasting time arguing out here? Frankie, I want you to keep hold of her and do not let her out of your sight."

He nodded and slipped an arm around Emilia's. Maria turned to Missy and did the same.

"We don't go in if you aren't attached to either of us. And you're not going up to that tower. Just the first couple of floors."

Duane watched the four of them intently and Maria felt bad that he was going to have to walk alone. He unlocked the door, carrying his huge flashlight. He was a sitting duck.

"Can you be a dear and show us where your daughter was last seen?" Missy asked Duane and he nodded. He stepped inside, shining the beam around the dark space. Missy and Maria followed behind and the elderly woman let out a gasp, holding up her hands.

"I can hear you all," Missy whispered. "One at a time, please, and I will help, but first of all I need someone to come forward and help me. Who knows what's going on inside this place? Who can tell me what I need to know?"

Her voice was soft but firm. Maria could sense them, so many souls hovering in her peripheral vision, shadows and blurs, lives wasted and trapped in this place. She glanced at Frankie who looked terrified. Emilia was watching Missy, a look of concern on her face that made Maria feel even worse for bringing them here.

"Thank you," Missy went on. "What's your name, darling?"

Maria squinted in the direction Missy was facing. She turned to Duane and mimed writing to him. He nodded and took out a notepad and pen.

"Frances, is it? It's nice to meet you. I'm Missy and these are my friends. Do you know why we're here?"

There was a stillness in the entrance of the hospital that Maria hadn't encountered before. The air felt full of static, like a distant humming in the background that was gathering strength.

Missy nodded. "That's right—have you seen the girl?"

Duane was open-mouthed and his eyes stared intently at the empty space in front of Missy.

"I thought so," she said. "Does it keep you trapped here? Is that why you can't move on?"

Maria heard a gentle sob behind them and turned. She saw a figure, its head bent low, with long strands of black, greasy hair, rocking back and forth, and her heart thundered. She was too terrified to move and disturb Missy who stood directly in front of her. A coldness seeped over her as the figure stepped forward and reached out to touch her. Fingers of steel gripped her arm and clamped it tight, and Maria couldn't stop the scream that erupted from her mouth. Missy, startled, turned to face her. Maria didn't like the look on her face as she held up one hand.

"Step back. I can help you, but you have to let go of her. She isn't yours to touch."

The grip tightened and Maria felt her lungs contract. It was so hard to breathe she felt as if life was being sucked out of her by the *thing* that held her arm. All she kept thinking was, *Please don't look at me, please don't look at me,* over and over, and then it slowly lifted its head. Maria wanted to tear her arm away but was frightened it would rip it out of her socket.

With panic in his voice, Frankie called her name. "Maria, Maria, talk to me. What's wrong, Maria?"

Somehow, she knew that if she opened her mouth, it would suck the last breath from her lungs and it would take her soul along with it. It had tricked them. The black shadow in the tower was a soul collector, but so was this creature. Were they working together? Or was the shadow only a distraction and this was what was really in charge?

Missy took hold of Maria's other arm. Her touch was so

warm and loving; so alive, unlike the dead thing that didn't want to let her go.

"Get off her now. I've asked nicely. She isn't for you."

Maria had never heard Missy's voice so full of anger.

"We came here to help. Now get the hell off her. She doesn't belong to you and neither does Riley."

Maria was stuck in a strange game of tug-of-war between life and love on one side, and death and despair on the other. The thing was about to make eye contact with her and yet she couldn't tear her gaze away. Its mouth opened showing rows of glistening yellow razor-sharp teeth. It tilted its head upwards. Two milky discs sat where eyeballs should have been and it was as if, against her will, they were drawing her toward them. The pain was so intense it felt like her insides were being pulled out of her throat.

When Maria thought she couldn't stand it any longer, it suddenly stopped, and she felt the life whoosh back into her body. Her knees buckled and she crumpled to the floor, gasping for breath. Looking up, she saw Missy standing in front of the thing as the creature gave a long, high-pitched howl. Missy stood her ground and the fear Maria felt for her friend was overwhelming. *Take me, not Missy*, she thought desperately.

Missy held her rosary beads toward the beast and shouted, "Take us to the girl or tell us where to find her."

There was a brilliant flash of light so powerful that it burned Maria's vision and for a moment she thought that lightning had struck the building. Then the light was gone, bathing them in shadows once more, and the creature had vanished. Still clutching her rosary beads, Missy stared at the space it had occupied only seconds ago with a look of both terror and astoundment.

Frankie bent down and helped Maria to her feet. Dampness seeped through her trousers, and she realized that she'd fallen into one of the disgusting puddles of stagnant rainwater.

"Hey, are you with us, Maria?" Frankie waved a hand in front of her eyes, but she could hardly blink.

What had just happened? In the space of two days, two different paranormal entities had attacked her in this awful place. Poor Riley hadn't stood a chance. Duane's eyes were glassy as he stared at the space the thing had occupied moments ago.

Maria reached out for him. "You saw it?"

He nodded once, then opened his mouth, but no words came out.

It was Emilia who took charge. "Out. I want everyone out of here while we can still get away. We can regroup and figure out what the hell is going on here."

No one argued, not even Missy, who was the most stubborn of them all. They stepped outside into the cool mid-morning air. Maria didn't think she'd ever been so grateful as she breathed in deeply, trying to calm herself down. She didn't dare look back at the hospital, too afraid of what she might see staring back at her.

TWELVE

Sammi Jo had been up at the crack of dawn. She couldn't sleep after the events of the night before. How had that detective managed to grab his friend before she plummeted to her death? The scene kept replaying on a loop inside her head. If he hadn't reached her, she would have smashed through the rotting wooden porch to her death. It made her shudder just thinking about it. And where the hell was Riley?

She decided to pay her Aunt Dolores a visit. Nobody knew that hospital better than she did. She hardly ever spoke about working there, not unless she had to. But when she'd found out that Sammi Jo was going to be taking care of the buildings, she'd sat her down and given her a rundown on what kind of place it was. At first, Sammi hadn't taken her too seriously. But as time went on and she saw and heard things that couldn't be explained, she realized that her aunt was telling the truth.

Her tires crunched along the narrow gravel driveway, alerting her aunt to her arrival. She was already outside on the porch, huddled in her bathrobe, her arms folded across her chest, waiting for Sammi Jo, who got out of the car and waved at her.

"Morning, Aunt Dolores."

Dolores shook her head. "What in God's name are you doing here this early, Sammi Jo?"

Sammi Jo couldn't help but grin. Her aunt never changed. "Sorry, I know it's too early to be calling on you, but I need to talk to you about the hospital."

Her aunt's exhale was epic. "I knew it. I knew that it was going to be nothing but trouble when you agreed to take care of that wreck. I told you it needs burning to the ground and it still probably won't be enough to cleanse that whole area."

Dolores walked inside the farmstead. It was Sammi Jo's favorite place ever, so homely and modern at the same time. Her aunt had come into money a long time ago, after receiving a large sum most unexpectedly from some famous person who she'd taken care of at the hospital, and she'd spent it wisely. After buying this place and renovating it, she'd carried on working at the hospital until the day its doors were closed and the windows were boarded up. Dolores didn't like to talk much about her old workplace or her benefactor, but she said she'd been blessed, and in return she did the only thing she could do, which was to carry on helping the poor souls in her care as long as she could.

Sammi Jo sat down in one of the big comfy armchairs and waited for Dolores to pour them both a mug of fresh coffee. Her aunt made the best coffee she'd ever tasted. Taking the hot mug, Sammi Jo wished that she didn't have to go prying into the kindly woman's past and bring up memories she'd rather forget. Taking out her phone, she found the picture of Riley Holt and passed it to Dolores.

"Do you recognize this girl? It's Chief Holt's daughter. She went missing three nights ago in the hospital."

Dolores squinted, pulled the phone near to her face, then held it away. Standing up, she went to the kitchen to get her glasses. When they were on, Sammi Jo handed the phone back.

As soon as she saw Riley's smiling, happy face, she let out a high-pitched gasp. "Where on earth did you get this?"

Sammi Jo tilted her head. "What do you mean? I got it from the missing person's poster that's all over town."

Dolores shook her head. "Sammi Jo, are you fooling me, child? Why would you do something like this?"

Now she was confused. "I'm not fooling you. Riley went into the hospital with three friends the other night on some stupid ghost hunt and never came back out."

Dolores looked from the picture on the phone to Sammi Jo and whispered, "It's her... She's even wearing the same red sneaker. Well, I'll be damned." She looked at Sammi Jo, her eyes wide with wonder. "Am I dreaming, or are you really here? Or am I having some kind of nightmare, because I haven't thought about this girl for years..." She leaned over and touched Sammi Jo's shoulder. "Damn, I guess I'm not dreaming then."

"Dolores, you better tell me what you know. Then I can call the chief to come listen to it, too."

She shook her head. "You better call the chief to come over here right now because I'm not repeating myself. I'll tell you this tale once and then I won't speak of it ever again. I promised Miss Miller that this was between us. And it don't feel right talking about this even after all this time and even though she's been dead over fifty years. There are just some things you don't gossip about."

Sammi Jo smiled patiently at her aunt. "Dolores, if a patient has been dead over fifty years and you know something about Riley, who is in trouble now, then I need you to tell the chief everything. We don't keep secrets when it's about a missing teenager, even if you did swear to a vow of secrecy."

"Honey, it wasn't a vow of secrecy. It was a vow of respect and friendship. I only knew Miss Miller for a few days, but we got on like a house on fire. And I helped her, just like I would have helped anyone in that situation. But she didn't forget me, and I don't know how or why but when she left me money after her tragic death, I promised her that I would put the money to good use and not fritter it away. Breaks my heart to this day that I couldn't help her when she needed it the most." Dolores lifted a tissue from her pocket and dabbed at her eyes. "Call the chief and we can talk about it together."

Sammi Jo took out her phone and rang Duane. It went straight to voicemail, so Sammi Jo left him a message telling him to phone her back or, even better, to come to Dolores' house as soon as possible. She hung up and gave what she hoped was a reassuring smile to her aunt, who looked as if she had the weight of the world on her shoulders.

DECEMBER 1960

Faye was escorted back to her room after speaking with Doctor Becker. She smiled at the nurse, who hadn't made eye contact with her, and waited until she left her alone before she slipped next door to see the girl. It had been hard talking to the doctor, trying to sound as if she was sane, when all she kept thinking about was the girl telling her she was from a different time. One of them was nuts and Faye didn't want to take bets on which of them it was.

Before she did anything else, she opened the desk drawers and found some headed writing paper. She laughed. Boy, Joe was going to have the shock of his life when he opened this letter. But he'd come get her, anyway. He might not be her husband anymore, but he was still her friend, which was more than could be said for Arthur. She suspected it had been his idea to tell Doctor Friskle she needed a mental health assessment, though she didn't know for sure. The letter was short and to the point.

Dearest Joe,

I'm in this hospital full of people who are nuts. They think I'm nuts, too, but I'm not. I know Arthur is sleeping with his assistant and I'm sure he just wants me out of the way. I don't belong here. They even put me in a padded cell, until a wonderful nurse helped to get me out of there and into a guest room on the second floor, but I don't need to be here. Please come get me.

Yours MM xxx

She tucked it into an envelope and printed his address onto it in small capital letters, then slid it into her pocket ready to give to Dolores next time she saw her. She stepped into the corridor, which to her relief was empty. A door opened further along and the woman who'd just arrived yesterday stepped out. Faye smiled at her then slipped into the girl's room before she could get caught up in conversation. Closing the door, she found her sitting on the bed, and she lifted a finger to her lips to tell her to be quiet, in case the woman heard their voices and decided to join them. Then she crept across to the bed and sat beside her.

"Do you mind if I join you?" she whispered. "I don't like it on my own and I don't want to have to talk to the woman a few doors down. She scares me, she looks so intense."

The girl nodded shyly. "You can sit here as long as you want."

"Thank you. Now, have you figured out how you're going to get back home yet? Or did I make up that conversation and I really am nuts like everyone thinks?"

"You didn't make it up and you're not nuts. I was dreaming about my dad last night and heard him calling out for someone called Riley. So, I guess that's my name."

"Riley." Faye was deadly serious and looked her straight in the eyes. "I love that name. It's nice to properly meet you,

Riley." She looked down at her hands. "Look, honey, I've been thinking and I'm sorry to say it, but I think that just maybe you might be completely nuts. Because I don't see how you can be sane believing you're from the future. How could you have time travelled here?"

Riley shook her head. "I don't know how it happened, but I promise you I'm not crazy and neither are you. I think I was in this place with my friends. It was dark, and it was a wreck. In my time, this hospital has been abandoned for decades. We were ghost hunting and filming the place before it gets knocked down to build luxury houses. I saw a scary black shadow and the next thing I know, I was being dragged out of the treatment room, up some stairs to the tower, and then I woke up here. Everything was new. There were patients outside and I was wandering around with one shoe on, feeling as if I had the life sucked out of me."

Faye shuddered. "That's a terrifying story... I still think you might have been concussed from your head injury. Let me see."

Riley turned for her to look at a scrape on the side of her head, which didn't seem anywhere near as bad as Faye thought it would.

"Maybe I'm a little concussed," Riley admitted, "because I couldn't speak at first. I was so shocked, and then the nurses mistook me for a patient and said I had to stay here until they could find my family. How are they going to find my family? My mom and dad weren't even born until the seventies."

Faye gently touched her shoulder. "We'll think of something."

"You're not insane either."

"How could you know that? I'm an actress—I could be pretending."

Riley smiled at her. "You are a brilliant actress, but I also know that you spent a lot of your time sad and very lonely."

Faye arched one eyebrow. "How would you know that?

We've only just met. If you are who you say you are, then I'm probably dead long before you were even born, unless I'm some old lady living in a retirement village." She laughed but noticed that the girl was no longer looking at her and was staring down at her hands.

"You must know how I die, if you're from the future. I don't live that long, do I? Is it awful? Do I ever meet someone who truly loves me for who I am before I do?" She sighed. "Look at us, two girls stuck in a place neither of us wants to be."

"I don't know how you die," Riley began, "but I know that everyone loves you. I told you before that you're more famous in the future than you are now."

"That's not what I asked."

Riley squeezed her hand. "I'm sorry, I know very little about you. I haven't read up on your life. I've just seen the old movies and the photos—so many beautiful photos of you. I know who you are but nothing about you personally."

Faye laid her head on Riley's shoulder. "That's okay. I guess I'd rather not know how it ends. I could do with a friend like you even if you are a little kooky. We all need a friend in a place like this. It's not how my doctor sold it to me. She promised me I could rest here. I hate being lied to. When I get out, I'm firing her sorry ass. Do you think we'll get out of here? We need to think of a way to get you back to your real life, your family. You said that a shadow thing dragged you here. If that's what happened, do you think we could find it and ask it to take you back?"

The girl nodded. "Possibly. But I don't know why or how it brought me here."

"Maybe Dolores could help. She's not the kind of woman who takes no for an answer. She doesn't take any messing around; she would probably even scare that shadow thing to death."

Riley laughed. "She has been very kind to me, too."

"Maybe she could get us up to that tower and you could ask the scary thing in there to take you home. Then you can go back to your life, and hopefully Joe will come rescue me and take me back to mine."

"We could try. But I don't think you should go anywhere near the tower. I don't want to drag you into this."

Faye squeezed her fingers. "I'm already dragged into this, and besides, what else is there to do? It's not like we have onsite entertainment or can go to the bar and drink cocktails. I like you, Riley, and I want to help you, like Dolores helped me."

As if she'd heard her name, the door opened and Dolores entered, closing it behind her.

"What a beautiful pair you both make. Faye, I'm going off shift soon—did you manage to write that letter?"

Faye jumped off the bed and pulled the envelope from her pocket. "I did, thank you. Before you go, we need to talk to you about her predicament, don't we, Riley?"

Riley nodded, so Faye continued, "Dolores, I know you work with poorly people all day long and this is probably going to sound wilder than you can imagine. But this girl swears it's the truth and, do you know what? I believe her, a hundred percent."

Dolores smiled at them both. "Go on, I'm listening."

Faye looked at Riley. "Should I tell her, or will you?"

The girl pointed to Faye, who turned back to Dolores.

"Riley isn't from here."

"I know that, child. I figured it out as soon as I set eyes on her."

"You did?"

Dolores nodded.

"But it's not like she's from out of town or another state. Well, the thing is, she's from the future." Faye held her breath for a moment while her words sank in. "She shouldn't be here, but some scary shadow thing dragged her out of her time. It lives in the tower, we think. We're planning to go up to the tower and ask it to take her back."

"You're... planning what?"

Faye smiled innocently. "How else can we get her back home?"

The nurse folded her arms across her chest. "The pair of you are serious? Time travel, evil shadows...? You're willing to talk about this to me, even though you could get locked up in here for life for sharing crazy theories like this?"

They nodded uncertainly in unison.

"You don't know how lucky you are that you told me about this and nobody else." She glanced at the door. "We don't talk about *the shadow* in front of the patients. The doctors won't acknowledge that it's real, but we've all seen it, or felt its presence. I call it the soul collector. It lingers around when a patient is about to die, waiting in the corner of rooms for their souls. Or at least I'm convinced that's what it does."

It was Faye's turn to look shocked. "Dolores, are you for real? This is starting to sound like some weird movie script, not real life."

"I'm deadly serious, Miss Miller. That thing has been lurking around since before this place was built, I'm sure of it. Now with this hospital here it has the perfect hunting ground, and it won't ever leave on its own." Dolores looked sympathetically at Riley. "I don't want to sound pessimistic, but I don't think it will let you leave either."

She shook her head. "Time travel? That has thrown me, I have to admit. All I can think is that something must have gone wrong when the shadow tried to take you, dear. I don't know what happened, or why, but if you promise me you're telling the truth, then I'll believe you. My guess is that the creature, whatever it is, can move between time and space, which is more than I can get my big, old brain around. It wanted your soul, Riley, but ended up bringing you here, instead. I don't know how we're going to fix this, I really don't. But I will go home and think about it and see what I can come up with."

Faye rushed across the room and threw her arms around Dolores, who laughed but also gave her the biggest hug that she could muster. Faye closed her eyes. The love and warmth this kind woman exuded was enough to save anyone's soul. She just hoped it could save the girl's.

THIRTEEN

Frankie followed the chief's pickup to Sammi Jo's aunt's beautiful small farmstead. Getting out the car, Maria smiled at the chickens wandering around the yard. There was a dog watching them silently from his spot by the front door.

"Some guard dog that is." Frankie bent down and scratched the dog behind its ears. He loved dogs and had told Maria that if he hadn't joined homicide, and if Christy hadn't been allergic, he'd have been a dog handler.

Duane hammered on the front door a little too forcefully. The door opened and Sammi Jo greeted them. "Oh, I see it's a coach party. Come on in, Dolores has coffee on." Maria gestured to Missy and Emilia, who were waiting in the car, and Sammi Jo nodded. "Absolutely, everyone is welcome here."

They all filed into the bright, warm kitchen-diner where the elderly woman was making a pot of coffee. Dolores walked straight for the chief, arms open, and pulled him in for a hug. It seemed to take him by surprise, but he didn't pull away. In fact, Maria watched as Duane melted into the woman's arms. She figured he'd needed that embrace more than he realized. When they finally pulled apart, Dolores pointed to the large pine table.

"Please take a seat," she said. "I'll serve the coffee, and we'll think about what we're going to do about this mess."

Missy looked around. "You have a beautiful home, Dolores. Thank you for inviting us in."

Dolores smiled. "Thank you. It's my pleasure."

The chief didn't sit. He leaned against the wall with his arms crossed. Dolores passed him a mug of coffee first. "Chief, you need to sit down for what I'm about to tell you. I know you're all kinds of upset and rightly so, but this is a hard tale to tell."

Duane did as he was told. Dolores winked at Sammi Jo who took over pouring coffee and passed the mugs around. Dolores sat in between Maria and the chief. When Sammi Jo finally sat down, and all the coffee was served, Dolores began.

"At my age, my memory isn't what it used to be, but it's good enough to recall this story exactly as it happened. And chief, you're not gonna want to hear it or believe it. I found it damn near impossible to get my head around it myself, at the time. I never believed that I would live through it twice and from both sides of the story."

Maria could tell the chief was desperate for her to get to the point, but he was too polite to rush her.

"I worked in Beacon Hill for my entire career, from when I qualified until the day it closed its doors for good. I saw every side of humanity there is to see. I nursed paupers and millionaires, even movie stars, and I never treated any of them different. I believe that we all deserve love, compassion and empathy no matter how big or small a person's bank account is."

She stalled, while gathering her thoughts and forcing herself to remember the strange tale she was about to share with them. "What I'm about to tell you is going to sound as if I should have been a patient there myself. But all I can tell you is it's the truth. I have no reason to make stuff up and I'm too old and tired to even try, especially when it involves your daughter, chief, who I met for the first time on December second, nineteen-sixty."

Maria couldn't hold back her gasp. The chief stared at Dolores, shaking his head. Frankie was open mouthed, while Missy and Emilia straightened in their chairs, hands clasped in front of them.

The chief composed himself enough to ask, "You met my seventeen-year-old daughter, Riley, in nineteen-sixty?"

Dolores nodded. "I had no idea she was your daughter until Sammi Jo turned up here this morning and showed me her picture."

"What the hell?" The chief's politeness crumbled. "You expect me to believe you met my daughter in a mental health facility in nineteen-sixty? She wasn't even born for another fifty years. Hell, I wasn't even born then, so how do you figure that one out?" He stood up, put down his coffee cup, and Dolores met his eyes.

"I asked you to hear me out, chief. I'm gonna tell you exactly what happened and then you can try to figure it out yourself."

Maria grabbed his arm. "Sit down, Duane. We have to keep an open mind here, because nothing about Riley's disappearance makes any sense."

The broad man flopped down onto the chair with a thud. When she was ready, Dolores continued.

"Riley was found wandering in the grounds. Dazed, confused and scared to death. She didn't speak for the first forty-eight hours in our care, and nobody knew who the heck she was. She wasn't a patient, or a local runaway. She wore a single red Converse sneaker the likes of which I'd never seen before back then. Somehow, I convinced the doctor in charge that she could have been planted there to see what the place was like, to spy on us. He was the paranoid type, so he did what I told him, and we put her in an empty guest room up on the second floor where the rich people stayed. I knew she didn't belong there, but I didn't know any other way to keep her safe. Back then, we had some not-so-nice patients in the hospital, and I didn't want that girl to meet them."

Duane leaned forward, with his brow furrowed. "One red Converse?"

Dolores nodded. "We also had a very famous movie star up on the second floor. She took a shine to the girl and managed to coax her out of her shell. She gently convinced her to share her name."

Frankie was also leaning forward, intrigued. "Which movie star?"

Maria knew he was fishing for more details so he could do some fact-checking as soon as they left. That was fine by her, but she'd a strong feeling that Dolores was telling the truth.

"We knew her as Faye Miller. I've never spoken about her to anyone before. It didn't seem right. She was the most beautiful woman I'd ever met, both inside and out. I won't tell you her real name. Patient confidentiality never expires, in my book."

Maria knew the name Faye Miller from somewhere. She was sure it was the name that a very famous old Hollywood actress used whenever she wanted to keep her identity a secret. But she wouldn't pressure Dolores to confirm this if she was set against it.

"She was the sweetest, kindest woman and Riley loved her." Dolores crossed herself. "The pair of them became thick as thieves. She told Faye how she'd been ghost-hunting with friends in the hospital when some horrible shadow thing took her away."

The chief shook his head. "This is *insane*."

Dolores shrugged. "I warned you. Do you want to hear me out, or not?"

"Yes, of course but—"

Maria touched his arm again. "Let Dolores finish and we can figure out the rest after."

"Riley came up with a plan to return to the tower. She wanted to see if she could find her way back home, by tricking the shadow monster, somehow."

"You know about the shadow thing, the soul collector?" Missy asked.

Dolores nodded. "Ma'am, that *thing* still gives me nightmares. I believe it was there long before the hospital was built in Beacon Hill, but the patients certainly gave it plenty to keep occupied. After twenty years without patients, it must have been ravenous. Riley and her friends were probably too good an opportunity to miss."

Maria frantically scribbled down notes. "You're saying that the shadow thing, whatever it is, took Riley and somehow she ended up in nineteen-sixty?"

"Yes, ma'am."

"And that Riley and the actress became friends. Together they tried to get Riley back home?"

Dolores nodded.

Frankie rubbed his chin and Duane stared at his hands.

"Did they succeed?" Maria asked kindly. "Did Riley get back home?"

"Have you heard what you're saying?" interrupted the chief before Dolores could reply. "You really think that Riley is stuck in nineteen-sixty hanging around with some Hollywood actress? Are you being serious? We're wasting time."

Missy tutted. "Who are we to say time travel is impossible? I've seen many strange things in my time... demons, ghosts. Denying it is wasting time, if you ask me. We need to figure out how to bring her back."

The chief's phone rang. Shaking his head, he walked out onto the front porch to answer it.

Dolores shrugged. "I told you you'd find it unbelievable."

"Did Riley get back Dolores?" Maria asked again.

The elderly woman sighed. "That's the thing. I don't know. Faye's ex-husband, Joe, came to get her out of the hospital soon after. That was on December fourth, I'm sure of it. I'll never forget that day. It was chaos. He caused a real fuss down at the reception desk. He had two lawyers with him and bodyguards as well as news reporters. It was like something out of a movie. Though she wanted to stay to help Riley, Faye had no choice but to leave that day. But before she went, she gave her a ring of hers, a gold wedding ring from her soon-to-be ex-husband. In return, Riley gave her a plastic rose ring of hers. After Faye left, and the circus died down, I went to check on Riley and she was nowhere to be seen. I never saw her again, and I always assumed the shadow creature finally caught up with her. There was nothing more I could do."

The chief ran in. "That was one of my deputies. They took the dogs out again." His complexion paled. "They found a recently disturbed grave in the old cemetery. I have to go back right now."

Maria stood up. "We're coming with you." She turned to Dolores. "Thank you. If I have any questions, can I come back to talk to you?"

Dolores nodded her head. "I'm here all day, every day."

As they left, Maria's head span with the information that the old woman had just shared—and the possibility that it was all true.

FOURTEEN

When they arrived back at the hospital, a deputy who Maria didn't recognize was waiting by the entrance to the hospital. She paced back and forth, lifting her head every few seconds to look up at the tower. The chief rolled down his window and shouted, "Sally, what are you doing?"

Maria turned to Missy and Emilia. "I need you both to wait here until we know what's happening."

Duane was already out of the car. Maria and Frankie followed. It wasn't until the chief grabbed hold of Sally's shoulders to steady her that she finally looked in his direction.

"Chief?"

"Sally, what's going on?"

For a second her expression was blank, and Maria got the feeling the deputy didn't know what was happening or couldn't find the words to explain. "I... they sent me here to wait for you."

"Have they found a body?" His voice broke.

"No, just what looks like fresh dirt on a grave. But you know the local teenagers, they could just be fooling around."

Duane took off without another word.

"Can you show us the way?" Maria asked Sally.

The woman nodded. With one last look up at the tower, she shuddered and strode after the chief, who'd disappeared into the trees.

"You keep staring up at the tower," commented Maria. "What do you see?"

"I do? Huh... nothing really."

"Something was drawing your attention."

Fear crossed Sally's face. "Do you ever get the feeling something is watching you, but you can't see what it is? I thought I saw a dark shadow moving across that open window, then I realized I must be seeing things because how could I see a shadow from down here? I guess I'm just all sorts of nervous and on edge. I really hope there isn't a body in that grave."

Sally led them through the trees along a narrow, overgrown path that opened into a clearing where there were rows of misshapen wooden crosses, just as Abraham had described them. The chief was standing beside Walker. Ahead of them was a guy with a bloodhound and a mound of freshly dug soil. The chief was staring down at it, while Walker held his arm. This must be all his nightmares come true at once. Walker nodded in greeting and they both gave curt nods back.

"We need to get a forensic team down—" Maria was stopped by the sight of the chief falling to his knees on the mound of dirt. He began to dig through the soil with his bare hands.

"Duane, stop!" Walker shouted. "You don't want to be doing that."

Duane ignored him as his huge hands dug deeper and deeper.

Frankie sighed. "Crap, he's ruining any chance of good forensics."

Neither of them could stop him; the man was too big and too distraught. Duane kept heaving away the dirt until his hands reached something that stopped him dead in his tracks. Whatever it was, he tussled with it for several moments before he was able to lift it up. When his hand came into view, it was clutching a single red Converse sneaker. Frankie and Walker both darted toward him. Each grabbing an arm, they dragged him to his feet as he continued to clutch the shoe.

Maria felt her heart tear in two for the guy. But despite his agony, they still needed to do this the right way. "Duane, I'm sorry, but I'm going to ask you to drop that shoe on the ground and step back."

He stared at her. She didn't think he was aware of the tears running down his cheeks as he looked down at the sneaker in his hand.

"Is that Riley's?" she asked.

He nodded and his face contorted with pain.

"Duane, I'm sorry, I really am. I don't want to do this but if you want to continue to be involved in this investigation then you are going to have to put the shoe down and step away from the grave. We can't risk losing any more forensics. If you contaminate the scene even further, then we're not going to get any evidence from it. I know it must be so hard, but I need you to think about this for a second. If Riley is in there—and I hope to God she isn't—do you want to catch the person responsible for putting her there? Or do you want to let them get away with it, because we messed up the scene?"

All was silent except for the wind blowing through the trees as their branches swayed. There wasn't a single other noise, animal or human, not even the song of a bird. It was as if the whole world had stopped still at Duane's grim discovery.

Sally broke the silence. "Chief, should I call in CSI?"

Maria said that she should, but Sally waited for confirmation from her boss. Maria respected her loyalty. Duane swallowed hard, then he nodded. Dropping the sneaker to the ground, he stepped back. Frankie and Walker released their grip on his elbows, and he turned and headed back in the direction of his truck.

"I've got this," Maria told Frankie. "You go with him. Make sure he doesn't go into the hospital alone. Check on Missy and Emilia, too."

Frankie did as she asked and followed after Duane. "I'm not taking over," Maria said to Sally and Walker. "This isn't my jurisdiction, I know that. I'm just here to help and advise, so you guys get on with what you normally do."

Walker shared a look with Sally. "We appreciate that. Let me call in the crime scene techs and get this done right. We're going to need a pathologist."

Maria thought of what Dolores had told them less than thirty minutes before. "You might want to call in an anthropologist, too."

Sally raised an eyebrow. "Riley's only been missing a couple of days. She won't be that decomposed. God forbid that she's even in there."

"No," Maria agreed, "but it's best to cover all eventualities. If this was my scene, I'd call one anyway because this place is old and there might be all kinds of bones down there. They will take soil samples and work their magic."

Walker stared at the red Converse. "Sally, we need to run this by the book. Tell Dorothy to call the university and get Professor Greenwood to come down here."

Sally pursed her lips and for a second, she didn't move. But then she took out her cell and did as she was asked. She may not have liked being told what to do by a city cop, but at least she was discreet. Maria appreciated her tactfulness in not using the radio to call Dorothy back at the station, knowing that the chief would be listening in to their radio calls—and who could blame him? It's just what Maria would be doing if it were her kid who might be buried down in that cold, damp earth.

FIFTEEN

Maria looked around the overgrown, unloved cemetery. It had started to drizzle, like a curtain of tears falling from above for all the lost souls who'd been thrown into graves without a decent burial. No loved ones to say their last goodbyes, no friends to remember good times shared. It broke her heart to think that this had ever been allowed to happen.

The ground was soft for this time of year with the rainfall, meaning it was easy to dig down into the soil. Many of the misshapen wooden crosses were rotting and falling to bits. The clearing where the graves were was totally hidden from view, trees surrounding it on all sides, so unless you knew about this place it wasn't the kind of dump site you'd see when driving by. This meant that whoever had dug the grave must know the hospital and the cemetery well.

Maria closed her eyes and blew out a deep breath. How many patients had stayed here? How many staff had worked at the hospital in its time? The potential number of doctors, nurses, security guards, and caretakers over the years was overwhelming. Where should she start? Her mind went to Abraham, Drew's granddad. He may have been elderly, but he looked pretty fit for his age. Although she'd warmed to the guy, they couldn't rule him out as a suspect. He knew Riley well; he'd worked here. He'd even told them he'd dug most of the graves. He could probably find his way around the hospital grounds in the dark, blindfolded.

She needed to rule out the chief as a suspect, too, and sooner rather than later. His wife and her lover, as well as his daughter, were missing without a trace. Like Abraham, he also seemed like a decent guy, but who knew what was going on inside his mind? Then there was the story Dolores had told her. Was it the truth? Had she really met Riley at the hospital in 1960? Or was this story nothing but the ramblings of a senior who was potentially starting with Alzheimer's?

The crime scene techs were busy around the grave. The pathologist had declined to attend until they found a body, which Maria thought made sense. Everything was hanging on Doctor Greenwood turning up to excavate the grave. Leaving them to it until then, Maria made her way back through the trees along the narrow path until the tower of the hospital loomed above her. It was an ominous sight to behold. A shudder wracked her body as she recalled being pushed out of the window and almost falling to her death. If Frankie hadn't grabbed her... she shuddered again. She wasn't ready to die, not in a place as desolate as this, where her soul would be trapped for all eternity.

She found the chief in his truck, his head in his hands. Frankie was nowhere to be seen and neither were Missy or Emilia. Panic filled Maria so intensely that she couldn't suck air into her lungs. She took off toward the entrance of the hospital. The door was ajar. Without a thought, she pushed it open and ran inside calling, "Frankie, Frankie!"

Her voice echoed around the eerily silent entrance; her shoes crunched the broken glass beneath her feet. A loud bang from above made her heart skip a beat, but she carried on. She couldn't let her friends wander around in here.

God damn you, Frankie, I told you to keep them safe.

At the bottom of the staircase, heart racing, palms sweating, she put a foot on the first step and tried to muster the strength to carry on up to the first floor. Where were they? Wouldn't she hear their muffled voices if they were wandering around? Then she heard it. Slow, dragging footsteps from something much bigger than her friends. They were getting closer, blocking her from going up or back down. Maria opened her mouth to scream when she felt something icy cold press down against her lips, stopping her in her tracks. It felt as if someone had pressed long-dead fingers against her mouth to stop her from crying out.

A soft voice whispered in her ear, "Leave now, it's not safe. Your friends are not here, and neither is the girl. Time is running out."

"Maria, what are you doing?"

Frankie's loud voice came from behind her. Maria forced her body to turn around and saw him standing in the open doorway. She didn't wait another second. She ran toward him, pushing him outside into the cold, and slamming the door shut behind them. She couldn't speak, as if her words were as frozen as her insides.

"Why did you go in on your own?" Frankie demanded. "You told us not to do that."

Maria slammed the palm of her hand into his chest. "Where were you? I thought you'd gone inside with Missy and Emilia."

He blinked. "You've got to be kidding me, I'm not going back in there unless I really have to. We took a walk around the side of the building, so the girls could take a look from the outside."

She felt her rush of anger subside as quickly as it arrived. "The girls?"

He pointed to the back of the car where Missy and Emilia

were deep in conversation. In that moment, her heart filled with so much love for the three people who meant the most to her—and relief that they were safe.

"You douchebag, Frankie. Thank God you didn't take them inside. Whatever is in there, it's awake and waiting for someone to step out of line."

"Yeah, and you were about to hand yourself to it on a plate like a Thanksgiving turkey, all wrapped in shiny foil and ripe for the oven."

"We have to figure out what the hell is happening here and fast." She glanced at the truck where the chief still waited for news. "I think we need to check him out, get back to the precinct and see if Duane is above board. We also still need to find his wife and speak to her. If we can't find her, then it's not looking too good for him. We can also take the girls back and then at least I'll know they're safe." She noticed a new car parked by the chief's. "Whose is that Jeep?"

"The anthropologist arrived. Took one look at the grave and ordered everyone back."

"Should we go and see what's happening, then leave them to it?"

He nodded. "Lead the way."

They headed back through the trees to the cemetery where a woman dressed in full crime-scene attire was kneeling at the grave. There were a couple of college students standing behind her. The woman gave Maria a curt nod.

"You the city detectives?"

"We are. I'm Maria, this is Frankie, my partner."

"I'm not sure what's going on here. The ground has recently been disturbed, but it's obvious that this is an old grave."

"You know about the chief's missing daughter?" asked Frankie.

"Terrible shame. There's no smell of decomp coming from

here, no unusual insect activity and I think that when I get down to it, there isn't going to be a fresh body buried here."

"But the shoe the chief found was his daughter's."

"That may be, but my professional opinion is that someone is messing with Duane. It's a horrible thing to do, not to mention cruel. But I don't think I'm going to find his daughter in here. How long has she been missing? Two, three days? There would be definite signs of decomp if she was in here and I'm just not seeing anything. I'll excavate and we'll take a look at the bones or whatever else we find down there. For now, I can't give you more information than that." She frowned. "Why are you two here, anyway?"

Maria let Frankie answer. "I trained with Deputy Walker. We're old friends and he called in a favor."

"Well, I hope you find Riley soon. Duane must be beside himself; I can't imagine how his brain is even functioning at this point. I'd be a hot mess if it was me, unable to take care of myself, never mind come to work. He's certainly brave."

Maria smiled grimly, and she and Frankie walked back to the car. Was the chief brave, or was he clever? That was the billion-dollar question. If he did have something to do with his daughter's disappearance, his prints were now all over their evidence. There was also a handful of witnesses who could vouch for the fact that he'd held the shoe, making it inadmissible as evidence in court.

"What are you thinking?" Frankie asked.

With a lowered voice, she said, "That we need to clear the chief fast, and to do that we need to locate his wife and soon because we're wasting time."

"Let's get the girls back to the safety of their apartment and we'll get to it. I much prefer working with a tangible lead than running around in circles in that scary hospital. Do you think that old broad was off her trolley or telling the truth about meeting Riley in the sixties?"

"I'm torn between believing her and not, but I'll tell you another person of interest we need to take a closer look at."

"Who?"

"Drew's grandad. He worked at this place and knows it like the back of his hand. How do we know he hasn't been killing people for years? He had the perfect opportunity, with the freedom of the grounds. He was even the one who dug all the graves."

Frankie let out a long groan. "C'mon, it can't have been the old guy who makes the best damn chili I ever tasted. Don't do this to me, Maria. You're killing me slowly today."

She rolled her eyes. "Being able to make a killer chili doesn't rule you out as a suspect in a missing person's case." Her face paled and she cupped a hand to her mouth. "Oh my God."

"What now?"

"What if he ground her up and used her to make the chili? He could be full on Dahmer."

Frankie looked appalled. "Maria, stop it now. You're gonna make me barf all over my Italian loafers. Why would you even say something like that?"

"He was mighty keen to share his food with us."

Frankie held up a hand. "Stop it now, please. Let's run with the chief being our number one suspect for now, okay, and get back to the station to do some real police work."

Maria had to admit her theory about the chili was far-fetched, but as far as she was concerned, Abraham could still be a killer. Being elderly didn't rule him out, especially as he looked fitter than most men half his age. He'd been out working the garden when they arrived. If they could find a motive or a previous record linked to teenage girls, then they would be onto something.

SIXTEEN

Emilia and Missy refused to go back to the city, so they dropped them off at The Duchess Inn and Spa. Missy had done a quick Google search and found that it had a rooftop bar. They'd even managed to book a room with its own spa pool. Frankie escorted them into the lobby and then left them to it. Maria had begged them to reconsider and go home but they were having none of it. She'd at least managed to make them promise they wouldn't go anywhere near the damned hospital on their own. She knew how stubborn both women were—though even they weren't reckless enough to try something like that on their own. Frankie got back in the car and shook his head.

"I don't trust those two broads one little bit."

She laughed. "Me neither. I really hope they keep their promise."

He shrugged, starting the car. "The quicker we get back to the city and do some digging, the quicker we can come back to keep an eye on them."

. . .

They'd been given an office on the fourth floor when Lieutenant Addison had first asked them to run the strange crimes unit. Some smart ass had taped a poster of Mulder and Scully off the nineties TV show *The X-Files* onto the ancient wooden door. On account of these kinds of pranksters, they kept the door locked, so no one could go messing around in their files. Not that there were a lot of files, yet. Until now, their only case with any supernatural credibility was the demonic possession of the brownstone on West 10th Street. Since then, they'd looked at plenty of other cases that beat cops had passed on because they were weird, but it had always turned out that someone was behaving oddly yet the causes were perfectly human. They sent those cases right back.

Frankie unlocked the door, and Maria entered first.

"Ugh, what's that stink?" he asked.

"You mean it's not your feet?" Maria replied. "Did you leave some sneakers under your desk?"

Frankie flipped on the lights as his nose wrinkled at the offending stench.

"How dare you? That is crossing the line. You know how particular I am with my shoes."

Maria shrugged an apology; he was very particular about his shoes, and he always smelled of expensive aftershave. She looked around in the bins in case they hadn't been emptied, but they had, before checking underneath the desks to see if something had fallen off and was rotten. There was nothing. Frankie opened the blinds and threw the windows wide to let in some cool city air.

"Maybe the drains are backed up from the toilets and causing that smell through the air vents." Frankie was being serious.

"On the fourth floor? Won't gravity take the crap down?"

He laughed. "Not if it's blocked up here, it won't. So, bad

smell aside, I figure I'll go speak to Cooper down in Missing Person's. Do you want to start doing the checks on the chief?"

She nodded. Cooper was an asshole but him and Frankie got along well. He'd tell him far more than he would share with her. Plus, she didn't appreciate his wandering eyes that only seemed to focus on her breasts.

"Bring me a coffee back up from the vending machine because I am not drinking anything made out of tap water."

He frowned. "Maria, where do you think the vending machine gets the water from?"

"A separate tank?"

He opened his mouth then closed it, shook his head, and left the room. She knew he was only going because it didn't smell so bad out in the corridor. Having logged onto the desktop, she searched the records for anything related to Duane Holt and his wife. Nothing. To her shock, she found the chief hadn't even logged an official missing person's report for her. His wife had up and walked out of his life and he hadn't bothered reporting her as gone. That seemed kind of odd. She could understand him being angry with her for leaving him for another guy, but when he didn't hear from her, or she didn't get in touch with Riley for months, did he not begin to worry just a little that something was wrong? Unless it was like she'd said earlier. He wasn't worried because he knew exactly where she was, and he hadn't reported her missing because he didn't want investigators quizzing him.

This was difficult. How were they going to approach this? He wasn't the one who'd asked for their help. The only person who might have heard something from Louisa Holt was Riley, which brought Maria back to square one. She took a notepad off the desk and wrote the following names:

Duane Holt
Louisa Holt

Curtis Lowell
Abraham Dean

All these people were connected to Riley but there were only two still around to question. She typed Abraham Dean's name into the system and watched as a file began to load. A picture of a much younger guy filled the screen. He had the same eyes and smile; there was no mistaking him.

Maria gasped as she read through his file. She'd not been expecting to find that. Had the chief looked into Abraham's background? He'd a record for four counts of the unlawful disposal of a body from December 1960. There was little else on there because the records were so old. To find out more, she was going to have to go speak to Dorothy at Beacon PD to see if she had anything on file.

Maria squeezed her eyes shut. She had a headache brewing and was desperate to lie down in a dark room somewhere to process everything. Instead, she began to research Faye Miller, and anything she could find related to the hospital. Images of a distressed and exhausted looking actress filled the screen. She even found one that seemed to have been taken inside a hospital. *That poor woman,* Maria thought. She'd every inch of her privacy invaded; it was awful. An image of her with her ex-husband Joe, two big burly guys, and another with a briefcase, appeared on the screen. Maria zoomed in and she recognized the entrance to the hospital. Was she wearing the plastic ring Dolores had described? The photo was too fuzzy to tell. Had Dolores been spinning them a yarn to impress them? Or had she really seen Riley back in 1960?

As an afterthought, Maria looked up Malcolm Collins, the College Kid Killer, and read his file. He was a sick guy who had picked up his victims on their way home from bars a little worse for wear. His first victim, Ashley Parker, was found three days later by some kids playing down by the banks of the

Hudson River. She'd been bludgeoned over the head several times. A month later, when the news stories had died down, another body was found, again by the river. This time it was a guy called Justin Wright, same injuries. The police didn't connect the murders until a third body was found: Jessica Tanner. By this time the whole town of Kingston was in total fear that someone was picking off their teenagers one by one. Courtney Moon was reported missing three weeks after they found the body of Jessica Tanner, but her body never turned up. The cops were told about a weird guy who drove around the streets aimlessly. His car was registered to Boston. He'd bought it secondhand and not updated the driver details. Security guards reported a burned-out car in the grounds of the old Beacon Hill Asylum. They figured that someone was living inside the old place for months because several times they found the remnants of discarded fires and empty cans of food. Turns out his wife had left him and he'd nowhere else to go. She'd always insisted her ex-husband wasn't capable of such awful acts, right until his death. Maria couldn't stop the churning of her stomach. The thing that had grabbed her back in the entrance of the hospital had looked like a long-dead version of Collins.

She typed in the search engine, *Where is the College Kid Killer now?* She hadn't realized she'd been holding her breath until the headlines screamed in her face.

Malcolm Collins Slain in Prison.

She exhaled. Her hands shook. She had a horrible feeling that it had been his ghost that tried to take her soul.

Frankie burst back into the room, and she screeched.

"Christ, Maria, you scared me. What are you looking at that for? The College Kid Killer is dead. And tell me you didn't buy the crap about Riley being back in the sixties hanging around with famous actresses?"

Maria shrugged. "He may be dead, but it doesn't mean he

isn't at that hospital still. We can't ignore any theories, as far-fetched as they might sound."

He flopped down onto his chair, then passed her a sticky note with a phone number on.

"What's this?" she asked, still shaken.

"The jackpot. A phone number for Louisa Holt. You see, I prefer to concentrate on the suspects that I can physically touch and see."

She frowned. "How did you get this?"

"Cooper is a man of many talents. Louisa rang the missing person's bureau sometime back in 2020. Told them she'd left her husband who was a police chief, and she was worried about repercussions. She didn't tell a soul where she was going. Wanted this number passing on to her daughter, if she ever reported her missing."

"What?" She stared down at the sticky note. "Why didn't Cooper do something with this?"

"Duh, there was no missing person's report. What was he meant to do? He took down the number and stuck it in a file labelled *Louisa Holt* which literally had this inside it and nothing else."

Maria was shocked. "I suppose we should be grateful he managed to do that."

"Give the guy a break. The chief never reported her as missing. No one else gave a shit about her or Curtis running off together. Do you know how many missing person's reports come in each day?"

"I'm aware that we currently have six hundred and six missing persons on file."

"Right. Now ring that number and see if she answers."

Maria picked up the desk phone and punched in the numbers. It went straight to voicemail.

"Hi, this is Detective Maria Miller from Greenwich Village PD. I'd appreciate you giving me a call back as soon as you get this message. Thank you." She recited her cell number then hung up. "Here's hoping she checks her phone regularly and doesn't leave it turned off in a drawer."

"Look, at least it's a lead. The phone went to voicemail so she must still be using it."

"You did good, Frankie, thanks."

He nodded. She knew he appreciated a little thank you occasionally.

"Hey," she said, "look at this." She brought up the screen with the picture of a younger Abraham Dean and pointed to the charges.

"Holy crap."

"Yes, or something like that."

"What are we going to do?"

Maria sighed. "You know what we have to do."

"Are you kidding me? Can we at least eat first and get out of this place? It stinks to high heavens. Oh, and this time you're driving back, while I play on my phone."

Maria was happy with that plan. She wanted to forget about Beacon Hill Asylum, to go home, shower and drink cocktails with Harrison, who had sent her a message with six cocktail emojis and nothing else earlier. But she could never switch off while there was this much going on, and a missing teenager. It was never going to happen. Instead, she stood up, tugged on her coat and grabbed her purse.

SEVENTEEN

It was late by the time they got back to Beacon. Sam's had closed early. A sign in the window read, "Closed due to staff sickness." It left Maria with a bad feeling in her stomach, because Sam never closed early, apart from Christmas Eve. Even if he was short staffed, he'd run the counter and cook. His loyal customers, of which there were many, would wait in line patiently. She wondered who was ill, him or Marge? She took out her phone and messaged Marge, who replied instantly. "Sam has a migraine and couldn't carry on; he's gone home to lie down; business as usual tomorrow."

"What do you think's up with Sam?" Maria asked Frankie. "Marge said he has a migraine?"

Frankie was sipping the last of his McDonald's coffee and grimaced. "It happens to the best of us despite our trying to avoid them. Or maybe the guy felt like closing early for a change." He winked at her, and she thought about the fact that she could have had a cocktail drinking engagement instead of being caught up in this.

"What's that face for?"

"I don't like this place. The whole town gives me the creeps. It's like it lives under the shadow of that hospital."

"That's deep, very deep for..." He turned his wrist to look at his watch. "Almost nine pm."

Maria parked around the corner from Drew's house, as her phone rang.

"Miller."

"Hi, this is Louisa Holt. You left a message for me to call this number. Is everything okay?"

Maria's eyes widened. She hadn't expected to hear from Riley's mom so quickly.

"Not really. I'm sorry to tell you this, but Riley is missing."

"*What?* How? Did she run away from Duane?"

"Not exactly. Can I ask where you are, ma'am, and why you've never been in touch with Riley? Is she with you by any chance? If so, I need you to be straight with me. It would save a lot of time and police work if you could answer truthfully."

The woman's voice cracked on the other end of the phone. "Oh, God. No, she's not with me, I wish she was, but I totally messed everything up. Where is she?"

"I don't know—all I can tell you is she went into the old Beacon Hill Asylum with a group of friends and was the only one not to return. I think you need to come home, ma'am. I don't know what your relationship is like with your ex-husband, but I think he would appreciate you coming back and speaking to him regarding what happened."

"I can't face him. Not after what I did to him."

"Who you talking to, Lou?" The loud voice in the background was slurred and Maria knew a drunk when she heard one.

"Just Julie. Be right there, honey." She lowered her voice. "Does Duane want to see me?"

Maria had no idea. "I couldn't say, but your daughter is missing. I think he'd like to talk to you."

"I'll see what I can do. I made a mess of things, and I don't know how to fix them. I never even said goodbye to Riley, and I can't ever forgive myself for being so selfish. What should I do?"

"Come back so we can speak to you. Talk to Duane and help us with our investigation. What kind of husband and father is he?"

"A good one. His only downfall was that he's married to that goddamn job and spends more time at work than he ever did with me. He loves Riley and dotes on her. That's why I couldn't take her with me. I couldn't break his heart twice. Please don't tell Duane I'm coming. I'll have to get some money together, but I'll be back soon. If you find Riley, will you ring me on this number and let me know?"

"Of course."

"Thanks." Then Louisa hung up, leaving Maria staring at Frankie.

"She's not coming home, you know that, right?" He didn't blink. "She's got herself in a mess, probably pregnant with a kid she doesn't want. Her lover is a drunk and she doesn't want to face Duane."

The sigh Maria blew out was loud. "I know that. After all this time I can read a person as good as you can. At least we know Duane isn't a monster who chased her away. He didn't kill his wife, and he probably didn't kill his daughter either."

Maria got out of the car. They would interview Abraham a little more formally this time if he was there. If not, they were going to the station to request his files, or at least see if they still had them. It had been decades since his arrest and there was a good chance they hadn't kept hold of them. Maria was praying that Dorothy was the hoarding type and didn't throw anything away.

Frankie watched her. "Are we going too far, do you think? This doesn't feel right."

He sure did like the old guy. He was never usually this reluctant to interview a suspect. She had a niggling feeling, too, deep inside her stomach. It was this permanent sense of unease that had been there since they'd first arrived in this town.

"Let's see if he's open with us about his past record. If he denies it or isn't very forthcoming, then we can tell the chief and get his opinion."

Frankie grunted, which she took as his agreement. She walked across to the front gate and up the path until she was standing on the porch in front of the door. Before she could raise a hand and knock, the door opened, and Abraham smiled at her.

"I saw you two pull up. Wondered how long it'd take you to knock. Come in—no chili tonight, we've already eaten."

Soon they were sitting at the worn kitchen table.

"I take it there's a problem?" he asked.

Frankie was never going to do this interview, so Maria took charge. "There is, actually. I've been looking at everyone who is connected with this case and some stuff came up when I searched your name on the system, Abraham." She paused, hoping he would take it from there.

"I suppose that it did," he eventually replied, "even after all this time, huh?"

"After all this time."

He held up his hand. "Why don't you let me explain and you can take it from there? And can you please call me Abe? Abraham makes me feel old."

She nodded. "Please, continue."

Abe got himself a cold beer from the cooler. He offered one to Frankie, who shook his head, and then to Maria.

Abe sighed. "Guess you guys are serious if I can't offer you a little late-night refreshment. Look, I know it doesn't read too good on your police files that I unlawfully disposed of a body. But you need to know the full context before you judge me. I'm not blaming you for thinking the worst. Hell, I would be, too, if I was in your shoes. Back in that hospital there was a mortuary where they kept the bodies until they could be buried. It wasn't even a proper mortuary. They didn't do anything other than keep them on ice. It was nothing more than a walk-in freezer, to be honest. There was a kid who was there for a short period of time. She had no family—or at least nobody cared enough to come get her. And well... look, people died in that place all the time, and no one gave a damn about most of them."

Maria felt every nerve in her body tingle. Was he about to tell them that he'd also seen Riley Holt back in 1960? "What was her name?"

"I have no idea. I was the groundsman. I kept the lawns neat, trimmed the trees and dug the graves. But I know that she shouldn't have been there. It was tragic what happened to her. I heard that bitch of a nurse who was in charge say there was no point in reporting her death to the authorities. It would bring an investigation. So, she told me to burn her in the incinerator. Just throw her in with the trash like she hadn't even existed." He shook his head.

"What did you do?" asked Maria.

"I couldn't do it. I had already dug a grave for one of the wealthy patients whose body had been left unclaimed. I went and got the girl from that damn cooler, and I put her in his grave. I made sure there was a divider between them. I didn't just throw her in. Then I covered her up, told her the whole time that if her family ever came looking for her, I'd let them know where she was. I even made a wooden cross and carved the date that she died on it as a marker. When the nurse found out that I hadn't burned the body like she'd told me to, she rang the cops with some crap about how I'd buried a body I shouldn't have. They arrested me, told me to tell them which grave it was so they could retrieve the body. I wouldn't talk. I wasn't having her disturbed again, for what? That bitch would have made them put her back in the cooler after telling them some bullshit story that her family was going to collect her. Then she would have thrown her into the incinerator. She cared for nobody but herself."

Maria hadn't been expecting that. She released the long breath she'd been holding. "What happened next?"

He tipped back his head and chugged half of the beer he was nursing. "They charged me with whatever bullshit charge they could make stick. They never dug up the graves, said there was no point, and when they started to question Nurse Joy, who caused all this fuss, she backpedaled and said she'd got mixed up. It wasn't a wealthy patient, after all, it was someone with no family. Best to leave them where they were already, buried and at peace. Ha! You think anyone who died in that place is at peace? I'll bet you fifty bucks they're not, they should never have built that hospital on the old reservation. It's too near the Wappinger tribe's burial grounds and I don't think the elders particularly forgave them for it, either, if you get what I mean."

Maria shared a sideways look with Frankie, who stared longingly at the almost empty beer in Abe's hand. "Mind if I have one?"

Abe fetched him a bottle out of the cooler. Maria closed her eyes, squeezing them tight shut against the pounding inside her skull that was getting worse by the hour. She waited until he'd passed Frankie the cold bottle then asked, "The girl. This might sound strange. But did she look like Riley?"

Abe's crinkled blue eyes met her gaze. "I couldn't say. She was blonde or what I could see of her hair was. But when I saw her, she was a mess, dead, and it was a long time ago."

Maria swallowed. "How did she die?"

"Fell out of the tower window. Some reckon she jumped, and others believe she was pushed. However, it wasn't pretty, either way. Poor kid didn't deserve that. Ain't nobody deserves that kind of death."

"How long was she in the hospital?"

"Four long days. She arrived on December first and was dead by the fifth. I buried her on the sixth. I wouldn't forget the dates, not when I got a criminal record because of it."

Maria felt panic rising inside her gut, moving up to the base of her throat, making it hard to speak. If it was Riley he was speaking about, if she'd somehow been taken back in time, they had to find the time portal, or whatever it was, that she'd stumbled into, and bring her back home—before she fell out of that window.

EIGHTEEN

They sat in the car and stared out of the windscreen up at the chilly night sky, which was peppered with tiny silver flecks of stars. Maria thought she had a better chance of reaching one of them than of bringing Riley Holt home. It was hard to get her head around it, the idea that Riley really was stuck in the past. At the same time, it somehow made sense in a strange, warped way. She'd read an article once about alleged cases of time travel that had made some valid points, showing pictures of people dressed in modern-day clothes in photographs from the past. Just because the majority of people hadn't experienced anything like it, didn't mean that it wasn't possible.

Beside her, Frankie stared out into the blackness. "What are you thinking?"

"You don't want to know what I'm thinking."

"I don't," he agreed, "but we need to figure out what's happening and fast."

The moon peeked out from behind a passing cloud. She loved looking at the moon and checking what phase it was in. She hardly ever had time to watch the night sky in Manhattan given how many hours she worked. Her favorite places to catch sunset when she could were Brooklyn Bridge, the High Line and Battery Park. She couldn't wait for the warmer weather so she could take a picnic, a chilled bottle of wine and sit in Battery Park to watch it. Maybe she could drag Harrison with her; that would certainly count as a low-cost date.

"Earth to Maria. Are you listening to me?"

"Sorry. I was thinking about watching the sunset in the summer."

"Jeez, that's really helpful. Why didn't I think about that?"

Maria sighed. "I was also thinking about the case. Whether we believe it or not, whether you like it or not, there is definitely —to put it mildly—something weird going on here, and time travel might explain it. When the doc excavates that grave, she may find Riley Holt's bones. After speaking to Abe, I think that Dolores was telling the truth. Riley was dragged back in time by the same thing that tried to push me out of the tower. And I don't think it's a consequence that Riley ended up traveling to exactly sixty years ago. She disappeared on December first and that's when she first appeared in the past, and she died four days later. Tomorrow she will have been missing for over three days, and I bet anything that if we can't reach her before then, it'll be too late to save her. Somehow, she's experiencing time passing like we are, only sixty years earlier." She took a deep breath. She knew Frankie wasn't going to like this part.

"Go on..."

"The only way we're going to get her back is if one of us gets taken back by it, too. We have to do what those stupid kids did that night they broke in. Go into the hospital alone and act as bait. Draw attention to ourselves, so it comes to find us and hope to God that it can take us back, too. If I'm right, we'll find ourselves in nineteen-sixty before she falls from that window. We can find Riley and get her out of there before she is killed."

"You're not serious?" He looked into her eyes. "You are serious?"

"I'm not scared to try it." She realized then that those words were the biggest lie to have ever left her lips. She carried on trying to sell it to him. "If we get Missy and Emilia to help clear the way, I could go back and find Riley then bring her home. We'd need to somehow trap that soul collector back in nineteen-sixty at the same time. Then all those poor souls it captured will be set free. Then they can raze the fucking building to the ground. We will have stopped Riley from falling out of the tower and her bones won't be in that grave."

"No."

"What do you mean, no?"

He shook his head double time. "No, no, no. Not now, not ever, are you going in that place alone to do that kind of stupid shit."

She crossed her arms. "What's your plan then?"

"I haven't got one, except for maybe grabbing the girls and getting the hell out of dodge. We can't do anything to help, Maria. Nobody has to know about your stupid idea about time travel. We tell the chief the case is out of our league and that we've been called back to the Village. It's sad, but sometimes that's how life goes. We can't save everyone."

She stared at him in disbelief. "If you want to go back then fine. I already said, I'll go in without you. But I'm not leaving Beacon without at least trying to get Riley Holt back, whether you want me to or not. I couldn't live with myself otherwise."

"Maria, listen to what you're saying. You sound insane."

"This is non-negotiable, Frankie. You either help me get ready, or you don't, but I'm not leaving."

"God damn, you're insufferable."

She smiled. "This is your fault. You dragged us here to help, so you have to take half of the blame."

He turned the engine on and drove toward the chief's house. "I reckon the least Duane can do is give us a bed for the night, while you tell him your stupid idea and see if he can persuade you out of it."

Maria didn't disagree. She half-hoped that the chief would tell her it was never going to work, that the whole theory was crazy. But deep down she knew he would try anything to get his daughter back, even if that meant risking her life, or trusting in things he didn't believe in, and she didn't blame him one little bit. She didn't have kids, and didn't plan to have any, but if this had happened to somebody she loved, she wouldn't care about anything or anyone else except bringing them home.

The chief opened his door before they'd even got out of the car. His huge bulk leaned against the door frame, arms crossed, and Maria wondered if he'd insist on going back inside the hospital himself. They got out of the car, and he called out, "It's late. What are you city cops doing roaming around my town this time of night?"

"Trying to figure out how to get your daughter back," Frankie shouted to him. They walked up the path and he stepped to one side to let them in. "We need a place to get our heads down for a couple of hours before Maria can put her stupid, reckless plan into place. I figured you'd be good with us sleeping on the couch and on the La-Z-Boy."

Duane nodded. "What plan? Do you know where Riley is?"

Frankie pointed his thumb in Maria's direction. "Ask her. It's nothing to do with me."

Duane led them to his kitchen. "Get you guys a drink?"

"No, we're good. Listen, I don't know how open-minded you are and whether you're going to play along with what I'm about to tell you, but you need to listen before you make up your mind. It might sound as if I'm not talking sense." Maria watched his face to see his reaction.

"Whatever it is, if you think you can find Riley, I want to help. Do you know they found bones in the grave that had been tampered with? They're from the sixties though. They're not my girl's, they just can't be. It doesn't make sense."

Maria's throat closed up. "Do you believe time travel is possible?"

Duane laughed, a hearty chuckle that came from deep inside his belly. "You didn't believe a word old Dolores told you, did you? She's losing her mind, bless her. She means well but she's not as mentally sharp as she used to be. After all those years of looking after patients, she could do with some looking after herself now. It happens to us all in the end."

"There are too many coincidences for it all to be the fantasy of a woman whose memory isn't what it used to be."

He stared at her, with his intense blue eyes fixed onto her own, and she knew he was trying to figure out if she was talking crap. She met his gaze and didn't break contact, letting him cast his eyes downward first, with a faint, pink glaze on his cheeks.

"Are you talking Marty McFly kind of time travel or Terminator?" He laughed again but it was a short-lived sound that died on his lips. "You are serious, well, I'll be damned. I don't know what to say, Maria, except if you think Riley is somewhere in the past, how the heck are we going to get her back?"

"That part I'm working on. I think if I recreate the evening when Riley went missing and go up to the tower on my own..."

Frank shook his head but kept quiet.

"When do we do this?" Duane pressed.

Frankie glared at him. "You're not going along with this?"

"I don't see that I have much choice. If I can get my daughter back, I will walk through the gates of hell with no shoes on whilst the soles of my feet blacken and burn. She's my whole world and if I don't have Riley in it... well, there's not much point in carrying on."

Maria took hold of Frankie's hand. Wrapping her fingers around his, she clasped it tight. "It will be okay. Think of it as a controlled experiment, Frankie. One to go down in the history books."

Duane watched them. "Am I intruding on something?"

Maria smiled at him. "We're like an old, married couple, but no, as we told you, we're just partners and best friends. He doesn't want me risking my life because then he'd have to actually work for his paycheck. Before I do anything, can you put me in touch with any of the Wappinger tribe elders who might still be around? I'd like to talk to someone about the evil presence freely roaming around those hospital corridors before I face it."

"I can take you to speak to my friend Jimmy. He might be able to help."

"That would be great." She let out a loud yawn. It felt like she'd been working non-stop for days—probably because she had. "I think what happened to Riley might have also happened to the last victim of the College Kid Killer, Courtney Moon. She could have also been taken back in time. They might even be together." She yawned again. "Sorry, it's been a long day."

Duane stood up. "I have a guest room with twin beds you are welcome to use. It may be a little dusty. I haven't really been in there much. I have no call for visitors. You are the first two in a long time. If you want, I can make you some supper and you can hit the sack."

They followed him upstairs to the end of the hallway where he opened a door and flicked a switch, illuminating a small room with two single beds.

"Perfect, thank you," Maria said.

"Thanks for the offer of food," Frankie said, "but I'm going to hit the sack. I'm way too tired. Mind if I use your bathroom first?"

Duane pointed to the bathroom door. "Be my guest."

Maria knew Frankie wanted to be alone to process everything that was going through his head. She left him to it and went back downstairs.

"Do you have any cereal? I could kill a bowl of Lucky Charms."

Duane grinned at her. "I can help you out there. I also have Cap'n Crunch's Peanut Butter Crunch if you feel daring."

"The Lucky Charms will be great, thanks."

He took a bowl, box of cereal, milk and spoon then placed them all on the table in front of her. Then he turned back and got another bowl for himself, letting Maria fill hers before filling his own way too full. She shook her head. He'd be lucky to get a mouthful of milk in the bowl. Then the pair of them sat in silence, apart from the crunching as they dug into the cereal. Duane, who had purposefully not been looking her way, finally made eye contact with her. His deep blue eyes stared into the depths of hers.

"Why are you willing to do this? Why do you even believe any of this could be true, more to the point?"

Maria swallowed her mouthful. "Because as out there as this all sounds, somehow it makes sense."

He shook his head. "That's not what I meant."

"Then what did you mean?"

"Why would you risk your own life to try and save Riley's? You've never even met her."

"Isn't that what we do? Isn't that the whole point of being a cop and wearing the badge? To protect and serve?"

"Yeah, but this is more than that. If you're right we're talking about a whole different level of protecting and serving. You could be risking your life. What if you get stuck there in the past?"

"Here's the thing, Duane. I don't know if I am right about what happened to Riley, but I have a feeling that I am, so y'all just have to humor me. When the results come back from those bones, I'm pretty sure they are going to be a match for Riley's.

Because I think tomorrow night she will fall or be pushed out of that tower. Only it's already happened, sixty years ago. When the hospital staff found her body, they tried to cover their asses. It's only because Abe felt sorry for her that he didn't cremate her in the furnace like he was told to."

Duane scrubbed his chin with one hand. "I don't understand how any of this is possible." His eyes sparkled in the light with the unshed tears he was holding back.

"Me neither. A case I worked a few months ago opened my eyes to a whole different world that I never knew or cared to know existed. If a demon can live half stuck between worlds, trapped in the attic of a New York brownstone for over sixty years, then it's possible other things can slip between worlds, and times, too. Even your daughter."

Maria let out a huge yawn that she tried, too late, to stifle. Duane reached out for her hand. "Get some sleep. I don't know what the heck is going on, or why it happened to my girl, but I'm sure glad that you're willing to help me get her back."

NINETEEN

Abe took three bottles of beer out onto the porch with him. Wrapped up in his fur-lined boots and thick, fleece-lined parka, he sat on the rocking chair, staring into the night sky as he sipped each beer until he'd consumed all three of them and needed to pee. He'd been hoping that God would see fit to pass him some words of wisdom while he'd been sitting out there. Instead, all that happened was that he got a cold ass and even colder fingers.

Even with a fuzzy head from the beer he'd consumed, he'd made a decision. Whether he liked it or not, this whole mess linked back to him. He never talked about that place because he'd been trying to protect Drew. It was easier to forget it even existed that way. Just like he'd tried to talk himself out of what he was preparing to do but found he couldn't. He'd buried that poor girl in that grave because nobody knew who she was. Now he knew that she was his granddaughter's best friend, the girl who'd been there for Drew in her darkest hours. The realization that he'd buried her outside the hospital all those years ago made the tiny hairs on the back of his neck bristle with both fear and wonder that it could even be possible.

Tipping back his head, he swallowed the last mouthful of beer, dropped the bottle onto the floor and stood up. His bladder wasn't what it used to be. Once upon a time he'd drink any man dry and not need to pee every ten minutes. A wave of sadness rushed over him for his misspent youth. He'd never appreciated how good it had felt to be young, with nothing more in the world to care about than the next paycheck and where he'd be drinking that night.

Stamping his feet, which had gone numb with the cold, he went back inside the house to relieve himself. After washing his hands, he stopped outside Drew's room and lifted his hand to knock gently. There was no reply. Slowly he pushed open the door to see if she was awake with those EarPod things in, but she wasn't. She was tucked inside her duvet, fast asleep. He could see from the glow of the nightlight that she was dreaming. Her eyes kept moving and her fingers were twitching.

He loved the kid more than anything. He tried to imagine how he'd feel if it had been Drew that hadn't come out of that hellhole. He couldn't even begin to process how painful it would be. He'd lost his only son in an automobile accident. He couldn't bear the thought that he could have lost her, too. He also couldn't ignore the fact that if Riley was stuck in that place, that he might be the only one who could bring her back. He knew about the darkness that lurked inside that old hospital. And he knew the building and grounds like the back of his hand. He could walk around it with a blindfold on and find his way. It made sense that he should be the one to go back inside and search for Riley. He needed to look in the places that the others couldn't, or wouldn't, know about. He needed to go up in that godforsaken tower and see if that thing was still there.

Maybe he could convince it to let her go and take him instead? If it sent him back to the sixties, he wouldn't mind—especially if it made him young again, too. Being old wasn't what he'd hoped it would be. Everything hurt, he'd slowed right down, and a bottle of Bud to wash down a hamburger was about the most pleasure he got out of life these days. He would offer himself up as a trade if he could bring Riley back. She'd look after Drew for him, and he knew Duane would, too.

He went down into the makeshift office, sat down at his desk and wrote a letter for Drew, telling her everything she needed to know in case he didn't return. She'd be well taken care of. There was a trust fund from her parents' life insurance, and the house would be hers, too. It was enough money to set herself up somewhere away from Beacon, somewhere the nightmares couldn't reach out of the dark to touch her. Thinking of her in a place like that was enough to make his heart happy. He folded the note and tucked it inside an envelope, wrote *Drew*, and propped it on the desk. It was time to go.

Abe went to the small safe where he kept his most valuable possessions and took out the keys for the hospital. When he'd been fired, he'd taken them. He wasn't sure whether it was to spite them or in case he ever needed them again. Had he known all along that one day he'd need to return to Beacon Hill?

He'd once asked Sammi Jo if the locks had been changed and she'd told him no. The only addition by the new owners was a padlock to the main entrance. A padlock, he could deal with. He had bolt cutters in the back of his truck.

He pulled a deerstalker hat onto his head. It would be as cold as a refrigerator in that place. Then he picked up his thick insulated gloves and tucked them into his pocket along with the keys. Taking the truck keys off the hook by the front door, he looked around his home. It was the place he'd spent all those happy years with his beloved wife, watching his son grow up, before watching Drew grow up. She was so like her daddy it made his heart swell.

He'd had a good life, despite outliving the people who he loved the most. He couldn't complain. He'd loved more than most people and he knew he had been blessed. There was a set of rosary beads hanging on a hook behind the front door. His wife Laurie had been a churchgoer. He hadn't been, except for the main holidays, when he accompanied her, not because he believed in God, but because he believed in Laurie. He clasped hold of the beads and lifted them to his lips, kissing them.

"Laurie, darling," he whispered. "I know you're around. I need a little of your strength and faith if you could send some my way. If this goes mighty wrong, I might be seeing you soon, but in the meantime if you could keep an eye out for Drew and ask the good man himself for a little protection, I'd appreciate it."

He put the beads around his neck, tucking them underneath his shirt, then turned to take one last look around his home with a smile on his face and his heart full of love for the old place and its memories.

Nearing the entrance to the hospital, Abe's heart hammered against his ribs. He took a deep breath to try and steady it. He'd be no good to anyone if his old ticker decided to give out on him now. He was a little surprised to see no one guarding the gates, and although they were closed, they weren't padlocked. He took this as a sign he was supposed to be doing this. Maybe Laurie had cleared the way for him? That was fast work, he thought, grinning to himself.

The overgrown trees surrounding the driveway blocked what little light there was from the night sky—even the moon in all her glory couldn't penetrate the foliage. A sense of foreboding washed over Abe, but he kept driving. When the dilapidated building stood in front of him, illuminated by the truck's headlamps, he shuddered. He stared up at the tower and the one open window stared back at him. It was like a single black eye socket. He felt for the rosary under his shirt.

"Dear Lord, give me the strength to bring Riley home. Amen."

He grabbed the flashlight off the passenger seat and strode toward the front doors, where the padlock already hung open. All he needed was his keys. He felt for the biggest key, inserting it into the lock. He inhaled as it turned and the door swung open with an ominous groan, like a coffin lid being lifted. Stepping inside, he didn't bother to lock it behind him. It would make it easier for him to escape, or for the search team to retrieve his body. He lifted the flashlight and shone it around the entrance. The beam wavered in front of him with the shaking of his hands. Each step crunched the glass underfoot. So much for being discreet: the noise filled the entrance.

"Riley, honey. I don't know if you can hear me but I'm coming to get you, sweetheart."

His voice echoed. The beam of the flashlight caught a glimpse of figures standing on the stairs. They were still here. Abe instantly realized that all those poor patients he'd buried had never left, and this sent a wave of sadness over him.

"Hey, I don't know if you all remember me. I helped you on your final mortal journey, if that counts for anything. But I'm here to help. I won't hurt you or bother you none, and I'm sorry you're all still here. Breaks my heart to know you never left this place of darkness. So, let's see what we can do about that. I'm Abraham—some of you might remember me. I used to cut the grass out front, and I'd give you a little wave or pass the time of day with you. I'm here to find the girl. If you could help me that would be great. I reckon after all these years, it's time to bring the light back into this place and banish the evil. What do you think? Do you want to get out of here?"

He thought he heard whispers filling the air around him. They were so faint they could be mistaken for a breeze. He stepped into a dark stagnant puddle of dank rainwater and felt something tug on his left boot. Abe jumped back. What the hell had just tried to grab him? He skirted around the edge of the water, not wanting whatever it had been to get a proper hold on him before he'd even begun to look around. A figure with long dark hair stood halfway up the stairs, blocking the way up.

He climbed one step, then another, hoping the figure would move. It stood its ground. He suddenly remembered a patient. She'd wandered the halls with her head bent to the side like this, too, until she'd died in one of the treatment rooms at the hands of a doctor. He'd said it had been natural causes, but Abe had seen the marks on her wrists where she'd been strapped down to the bench whilst they administered their treatments.

Now, here she was, stuck forever. What was her name? He closed his eyes momentarily whilst he tried to remember, and then he whispered, "Margaret... Margo... Martha." He opened his eyes.

"Martha, is that you?" The head straightened slightly. "It is you. I remember you, honey. I buried your body after they killed you. I'm sorry. I should have told someone about what they did to you."

The head turned and as it did, the hair revealed the bone-white face underneath it. Her mouth opened, revealing rows of sharp teeth. But it wasn't the teeth that scared him. It was the white discs that used to be her eyes. This creature used to be a woman he knew, but he wasn't sure what she was now. She glided toward him, and he did the only thing he could think of. He pulled out Laurie's rosary and said the Lord's prayer. Whatever it was stopped and faded in front of him. He didn't see the outline of Laurie standing behind him, but he felt a warm sense of goodness and took that as a sign she was nearby.

He continued up the stairs calling out, "Riley!"

The only sound now was the echo of his boots as they thumped against the steps. No point trying to conceal his arrival; it looked as if the dark force at work here already knew he was here and had sent Martha to greet him. If his hair wasn't already silver, Abe had no doubt that it would have turned white after that little encounter.

He headed toward the treatment rooms, which were even creepier than downstairs, but he kept on walking toward the room that Drew had told him about. Reaching it, he shone the beam into the darkness. A cold chill settled across his shoulders as he imagined Drew climbing onto that chair and fooling around. She shouldn't have done that—not after those godforsaken patients had suffered so badly strapped to it. But she wasn't to know. How could she have known? Everyone who'd worked there had kept their mouths shut when they should have gone to the police. The shame of not taking a stand against the cruelty some patients endured weighed heavy in Abe's heart. Too many people had turned a blind eye, and it was unforgivable.

"Riley?" His voice was thrown back toward him. Abe strained to listen for some kind of reply. Would he be able to hear her if she was decades in the past?

At that moment a black mass advancing along the corridor caught his eye. *Dear God*, it was coming for him. Abe swallowed the lump in his throat. Now the shadow thing was on the ceiling. His eyes followed it up there. He had seconds to get to the tower door before it was upon him.

It had been quite some time since Abe had run, but run he did. He pumped his legs harder than he knew was possible as he took off down the hallway to the tower door. The shadow thing hadn't expected that. It scrabbled down the walls, landing silently on the floor behind him. The creature was much bigger than he'd ever anticipated, but still he kept running until he was finally there. With shaking hands, he slid the key into the lock. Too late, he realized that the door wasn't even locked as he fell through the doorway onto his hands and knees, winding himself.

He pulled himself upright and yelled, "Riley, I'm coming!"

From somewhere a long way off, he heard a cry for help. It sounded light years away, but he heard it.

The shadow being pounded the floor behind him as Abe took off up the steps, panting heavily, his lungs on fire. He was too old and too unfit for this. At the top, he had to bend over double to catch his breath. The thing chasing him burst through the opening and exploded into a thousand shadows, turning the entire room so dark he couldn't see the beam from the flashlight.

"I don't know what you are but I'm going to stop you. And the only way you can stop me is by taking me back to where the girl is."

Abe's voice was loud but trembling. There was a whooshing noise and Abe felt as if all the air had been sucked out of the room. He turned around frantically, trying to see where it was. And then he wished that he hadn't. The black mass was mutating and growing in the corner, a pulsating, writhing, undead monster that made his blood run cold. Abe did the only thing he could think of and instead of running away, like his instincts were urging him to, he ran toward it, arms wide and mouth open. He screamed as his body collided into the rotting, stinking mess of horror.

TWENTY

Frankie and Maria were up and ready to go. Duane had been up even earlier and had left them alone in the house but not without leaving a full pot of coffee on the go and a bag of fresh bagels.

"I feel bad. We came here without warning and told him the most unbelievable story about the danger his daughter is in. Then went to bed, and somehow, he has got up before the pair of us to make sure we had fresh coffee and breakfast."

Maria looked over her shoulder at Frankie who clearly didn't feel too bad because he was slicing open his second bagel.

"Where do you think he is?" she asked.

"Gone to get warrants to get us sectioned, if he has any sense."

"And what would you do if you were in his shoes? Would you give in, or would you try to open your mind and see things from a different point of view?"

At that moment Duane walked in followed by a guy wearing a cowboy hat, matching boots and a checked shirt. He grinned at them both then held out his hand to Maria. "At your service, ma'am I'm Jimmy Two Trees." She took his hand and shook it firmly. He released her, then he greeted Frankie.

"Great to meet you, Jimmy. Thanks for stopping by."

He shrugged. "The chief here don't take no prisoners. I had a little too much to drink last night and ended up in the tank, so he didn't have too far to come looking for me."

Duane shook his head. "Jimmy, I've told you before, you keep wearing those outfits and you'll get yourself locked up on account of offending the public."

Jimmy threw back his head and roared with laughter. "The chief here is jealous he can't pull this look off."

Maria smiled at Jimmy. She already liked him. He sat down next to her and picked up a bagel, nibbling on the edge of it. "The chief said he has a big problem and thinks I might be able to help. What do you want to know?"

Maria glanced at Duane who nodded encouragingly. "We think there is some ancient dark spirit that is stalking the halls of the old hospital. I think that it likes to collect souls, that it's keeping the patients who had the misfortune to die there trapped. I also think it can travel back through time."

Jimmy chewed on the bite of bagel he'd taken whilst she was talking. "Before they built that hospital, there was a Wappinger burial mound on that site. We were moved on but there were stories about the land around there and the spirit-souls who bore great powers. Even those that could move through time."

"What does that mean?" Frankie asked.

Jimmy glanced at the chief. "My Kshotha loved to tell tales around the firepit in her back garden. Under the skies of the full moon, she would relay ancient tales so that we didn't forget who we were or where we came from. She talked about the Atlantoh, a great evil spirit with a destructive personality who could cause death. My Kshotha used to tell me it would come in the night and steal my soul if I was a bad boy."

"I've never heard of it." Maria said.

"Maybe you know its more recent name. Or the name it goes by since the Christians tried to teach their ways to the tribes. They would refer to it as the devil."

Every nerve ending in her body fired at once, causing her to jolt forwards. She closed her eyes. Why did it have to be something so terrifying?

Duane asked, "How do you fight it?"

Jimmy shrugged. "No idea, man. It's not something you'd want to do."

"It's a matter of life and death, Jimmy. If Maria is right, that thing took my daughter and she's stuck in nineteen-sixty with only hours left to live."

Duane's phone rang and he answered it, "Holt." He went to the next room, leaving Frankie, Maria and Jimmy around the table.

Jimmy asked, "Are you guys for real? This isn't some kind of bullshit story?"

Maria sighed. "I wish it was, Jimmy, I truly do."

"Maybe you can trap it, but you would have to get it at its weakest point. I don't know anything about how to stop the Atlantoh, and my Kshotha isn't here to help you. How would you fight the devil if you had to? Think of it that way."

"I'd rather fucking not," growled Frankie.

"We have Missy and Emilia. They can perform a ritual and cleanse the hospital. We haven't got a priest, but I don't think that's what we need. Jimmy, can you perform any kind of ritual to cleanse it or trap it?"

"Damn, I knew you were going to ask me that."

"Can you?"

He shrugged. "I can try. My father and grandfather were shamans. They'd take me with them to anything that needed cleansing when I was a kid, but it's not something I'd want to do if I could help it."

"Riley's life depends on it. That thing already tried to push me out of the tower window. You only need to keep it trapped back in time while Missy and Emilia try to close the window or portal that it uses. Do you think you can do it?"

The chief walked in. His face was ashen. "That was the doc. She fast tracked the DNA sample from the bones she recovered from the grave." His face crumpled. "They are a match for Riley... they are my daughter's bones. But they're sixty-three years old. How the fuck did my seventeen-year-old daughter die back in nineteen-sixty, when she's only been missing three days? There were also other bones with her... Hers wasn't the only skeleton they found."

Maria took a deep breath. "I think that those bones belong to Courtney Moon. Her body was never recovered, yet the other victims of the College Kid Killer were. I don't think Riley is the first person this has happened to on the grounds at Beacon Hill Asylum. Who knows how many we're not aware of? Homeless people, runaways, missing persons who may have gone in there for shelter and ended up losing their sanity and their lives in the process. We need to put a stop to this now."

Jimmy stared at the chief, then he turned to Maria. "I will do what I can. I need to get changed and grab some stuff. Where should I meet you?"

"The hospital. We don't have much time. Do *not* go in there alone. Wait at the gates and we'll formulate our plan before we drive up there."

He nodded then stood up. He glanced at Duane then back to Maria. "This is some weird shit. If I didn't know better, I'd think I was tripping." Then he walked out of the door and shouted, "Someone needs to drive me home."

Duane stood up. "I'll take him."

"We'll go get the girls from the hotel and tell them what's happening."

They all left Duane's house in a somber mood. The reality

of what they were about to face bore down on them, making them feel as if they were being crushed under some huge weight.

DECEMBER 1960

Riley hadn't slept. She'd laid awake thinking about how she got here. Mostly she thought about her dad and how much she missed him. She knew he'd be a mess. She thought about Faye, also. She felt bad for not telling her what happened to her in the future. If she'd told her about her death, could she have done something to prevent it? Riley didn't know. Maybe now she knew she died young, Faye would do something differently anyway.

Was Riley about to die young herself? She hadn't known she was crying until she'd felt the dampness of the pillow pressing against her cheek. It was all so unfair. She hadn't deserved this. Riley was scared about the thing in the tower. But if she didn't face it, what chance did she have of ever going home? Her best friend, Drew, would be worried sick, too; she'd lost her parents, and she would be devastated to lose Riley as well.

She turned to stare out of the window into the darkness of the night sky. The stars twinkled brightly, and the moon peeked above the tops of the trees. She wondered what would happen if she just walked out of the front door, ran through the woods and went home. It would be pointless, though, because that house wouldn't be her home for another fifty years. It might not even have been built yet, and her parents weren't born.

She lay there staring out of the window, watching the sky go from navy, to washed-out grey, then streak with pink as the sun began to rise. She whispered, *red sky in the morning, sailors warning* to herself. Was this an omen? Today she was either going to wake up from this nightmare and find herself back in 2023 with a severe concussion, or she was going to die. Whatever happened, she knew she didn't want to spend the rest of her life trapped inside Beacon Hill Asylum telling everyone who would listen that she was from the future.

Riley was still staring out of the window when a quiet knock on her door brought her attention back to the here and now.

"Come in."

The door handle turned and for a terrible moment she wondered if that horrible thing had come looking for her. *It probably wouldn't be polite enough to knock*, she realized. It would have appeared in the corner, mutating, growing bigger and blacker by the minute. The creature took what it wanted and didn't wait for permission.

"Hey, are you okay for me to come in?" Faye's sweet, quiet voice whispered through the gap.

"Yes, of course."

Faye slipped through the gap in the door. She was dressed in a pair of silk pajamas. Her blonde hair was mussed and her eyes looked tired, but she was still beautiful. She closed the door behind her and ran to the bed, clambering onto it beside Riley.

"I haven't slept all night. You don't look like you have either."

"I haven't. I'm scared."

Faye linked her arm through hers, and Riley caught a smell

of Chanel perfume—the same one her nan always used to wear, No 5.

"I bet you are. I'm scared of everything, but I don't have to worry about anything other than Joe coming to rescue my sorry ass and Arthur flirting with every woman he meets. Those things are nothing compared to what you have to face. Do you think that evil thing will take you home?"

Riley shook her head. "Why would it? It doesn't owe me anything. It's probably going to kill me, and I'll die before I can get back."

Faye's entire body shuddered. "Then don't go back, stay here with me. I can take you home with me when Joe gets here. You can live with me, and I could pay you to help with the house, although I already have a great housekeeper. We could find something for you to do. We could have so much fun. I could show you around Hollywood. We could travel to Europe, what do you think? I've always wanted to go to Paris and Rome with a gal pal to have some real fun. We could pick up a couple of Parisian guys and wear those little berets."

Riley closed her eyes. How wonderful would that be? To be best friends with Faye and travel the world with her. She could stop her from dying. She would be there for her like no one had ever been before... And then Riley felt her heart rip in two as a picture of her dad and friends filled her mind.

"It would be the most amazing thing ever. Like a dream come true, Faye."

"Then say yes. We could save each other. Don't you think that's why you were sent here, to save me? And maybe that's why I ended up here, to save you? If we save each other then we both get to live long, happy lives."

Tears rolled down Riley's cheeks once more and she tried to blink them away. Instead, she let out a loud, hitching sob that couldn't be contained no matter how hard she tried.

"I'm sorry, Faye. I need to go home. I miss my dad and my

friends too much. I don't think it would work if I stayed here. I would love to be your best friend and do everything you said, but I'd probably die of a broken heart knowing that my dad would never get over losing me."

Faye wrapped an arm around her shoulders and pulled her closer. "Then we will try to get you home. I was just being selfish. But if you get back and you don't like it, you come back to find me, and we'll go to Europe together. Promise me that you won't live your life unhappy and sad, settling for second best when you deserve everything you want."

Riley swallowed the golf ball in her throat. "Promise me you'll look after yourself and put yourself first, put men second."

Faye let out a loud laugh. "That's good advice from a teenager. I will do my best. It's not that easy here and now. Is it better in the future? Do you get to be you without having to compromise your entire life?"

"Yes, it is better. Women rock the world. We are prime ministers, global entrepreneurs, motivational speakers, you name it, we do it." Riley flexed her bicep and Faye giggled.

"Sounds fun and a little hard work."

"Not as hard as what you do. Look how far you've come. Do you ever stop and take five minutes to appreciate how amazing you are, Faye? How wonderful, talented and beautiful you are? Not just your looks. You are such a beautiful soul inside and out."

It was Faye's turn to sob. "Gee, you really are a breath of fresh air, Riley. Thank you, I will try to remember to do that. You say the sweetest things, even if they are funny and don't make much sense to me."

"Good. You better remember it because you are up there with the most inspirational women I know."

"Well then, we both better get our acts together. I was thinking, if you want to get up to that tower with Dolores to help you, I could go down into the reception area and kick up a stink, get everyone to come see what's going on, and make sure all eyes will be on me. No one will be watching what you and Dolores are doing."

"Do you think you could?"

"Honey, I'm an actress. It's what I live for." She flashed Riley the smile that filled every poster she'd ever seen of her, her blue eyes sparkling. It was as if she'd flipped a switch and turned from Faye Miller to a Hollywood star in the blink of an eye. She stood up and flounced around the room, then turned and bent forwards, her hands on her knees. Her hips moved to a beat only she could hear.

"A kiss on the hand can be quite continental, but diamonds are a girl's best friend." She winked and blew a kiss at Riley who clapped and laughed.

There was a loud bang as the bedroom door crashed open and smashed into the walls, making them both scream at the top of their voices. A streak of black rushed past the doorway and bile rose in Riley's throat. She raced to the doorway to see if she could find it. If it was here, it could take her back home now and stop wasting her time. But the only thing left in the empty hallway was the lingering stench of something rotting.

Faye stood behind her, holding onto her shoulders. "What was that?"

"I think it was listening or watching us from outside somehow."

"Was it the monster?"

Riley couldn't find her voice to speak, her throat was so dry. She felt herself pulled back inside and watched as Faye slammed the door shut.

"Honey, whatever that thing is, it's mean and it's scary, not to mention it stinks to high heaven. I don't think you should mess around with it. I used to think ghosts were something that lived inside here." She tapped the side of her head with a finger.

"Not anymore. This place is enough to either scare the crap out of you or send you over the brink."

Riley agreed with her, but she knew deep down she had no choice but to confront the shadow monster again. If it was watching her, why hadn't it killed her when it had the chance? She had a thought. What if it hadn't touched her because it was scared of her? Maybe it couldn't understand her, the way she couldn't understand it? If that were true, she might be able to use that to her advantage. For the first time in days, she felt a little bit of hope.

She turned to Faye. "I have a plan—well, it's partly your plan, but I know now how we can do it."

The pair huddled on the bed, wrapped up with blankets because the room was cold, and Riley whispered in Faye's ear, afraid that the thing was listening to them. If what she was planning was going to work, she had to surprise it.

TWENTY-ONE

Frankie was driving into town when he turned to Maria. "You called it. Hell, you knew those bones would be linked to this case. But how do the Malcolm Collins murders tie in with all of this?"

She shrugged. There was no pleasure to be had from gloating about being right over this one.

"He was pure evil. That soul collector probably gained a lot of power from his kills. Or maybe it was just an average Joe living in that hospital until he was influenced by that thing to commit the murders. Whatever the truth is, I think that when he died it took his soul and trapped him there. Maybe the voice I've heard telling me to get out was Courtney Moon's? Until we know for sure that her bones are in the grave with Riley's, it's hard to prove my theories."

"How though, Maria? Six months ago, you didn't believe in any of this kind of stuff and here you are like a goddamn psychic portal to the world of the undead. Now you're going to go in that hospital and try to trick something that has lurked around for God knows how long and sucks the souls right out of the dying to take you back to nineteen-sixty. Am I going mad? Are we really here or am I locked up on a psych ward on a Thorazine drip, tripping like there's no tomorrow?"

Maria laughed. It wasn't a cruel laugh, because she wasn't like that. But Frankie was right: what they were doing sounded out there. "You're definitely not tripping. I kind of wish that you were though because I'm not too stoked about the concept of trying to negotiate the holiday of a lifetime with some ancient, evil spirit."

"Yet you're still gonna try. What if you don't make it back, kid? I can't live without you in my life. I certainly couldn't do this job without you. I wouldn't be a cop if you weren't my partner."

"Frankie, I feel the same, I really do."

"Give me the big fat *but* that I know is coming."

"But we have no choice. Time is almost up. We have, what, a couple of hours before whatever is going to happen to Riley happens. We have to try to save her. I'm counting on you to make sure Missy, Emilia and Jimmy do something to trap that thing and stop it coming through whatever fissure in time it's using."

"What if we trap you back there, too? Then what, Maria?"

She closed her eyes; she didn't want to think about that.

"The sixties were pretty cool, not a bad time to have a midlife crisis."

"You're a pain in the ass and not funny at all."

"Let's just see how it goes. It might not even work."

"I hope that it doesn't." Frankie's voice was strained.

"You don't mean that. You want Riley home as much as I do."

He didn't say another word until he reached the parking lot of the hotel. "What if Missy tells you no?"

"She won't. She will want us to at least try."

"Why are you broads so stubborn?"

Maria laughed. "I'll go get them; you wait here."

She was out of the car before he could disagree. She wanted to speak to the women and hear what they truthfully thought her chances were without Frankie listening, because if he heard them say that they were bad, he'd end up cuffing her and dragging her back to Manhattan.

Through the bustling hotel entrance, she saw Missy and Emilia waiting for her. She pulled them both into her arms and squeezed them as tight as she could without hurting them.

"Uh oh, what's going on, Maria?" Missy asked. She wasn't a fool and could read her like a book.

"We have a plan. I need you to tell me if it's ridiculous or not?"

Emilia stared at her. "Sweetie, it is. I can tell you that now."

Missy smiled at Emilia. "Honey, let's hear it first."

Maria gave them a quick rundown, her eyes flicking from one woman to the other, trying to read their thoughts. When she'd finished, Missy blew out a long breath. "That's some plan."

"I know. I need to know what you honestly think."

"It's foolish and dangerous. I don't know how you expect to go back in time and then find your way back before we seal that tower and bless it with love and light."

Missy was always straight talking, and Maria felt her heart sink. "Not even if Jimmy helps?"

"Not even if the whole Wappinger tribe were helping. But I suppose like anything there is the slightest chance that by the grace of God it could work, and you could find the girl and bring her back. I mean, none of us know what we're doing really. Nobody ever gave us a rule book on how to deal with demons or the supernatural. We do it and hope for the best. I guess this is no different."

"That's good enough for me. Please don't mention to Frankie you think that it's foolish and this is nothing more than a suicide mission. I have to do this for Riley's sake, and my own.

I couldn't sleep at night ever again knowing that I didn't at least try."

Missy nodded. "In that case I think it's a fabulous idea and you should put it into action sooner rather than later." Missy linked her arm through Maria's and Emilia's. "Come on, let's get this show on the road. We're going to need to stop off at a church for some holy water and a quick blessing, if there's one on the way."

"We'll find one."

They pulled their case along behind them and walked to Frankie's waiting car. He jumped out when he saw them, before popping the trunk to lift their bags in.

"Morning to my two favorite ladies. I hope you've told Maria that she is being stupid."

Missy kissed Frankie's stubbled cheek. "Actually, dear, we think it's a great idea as long as we have lots of holy water and a little luck."

He shook his head as he lifted the cases in. "She told you to say that, didn't she?"

"Don't be presumptuous, Frankie, of course not."

He grunted at all three of them. The two ladies smiled sweetly, their fears tucked deep inside their hearts so he couldn't see them, and Maria felt a rush of love so strong and pure. She knew she could draw on their love if she ever needed strength to make it back.

TWENTY-TWO

The house was silent when Drew woke up, but she assumed it was because her grandpa had gone out to do some errands or help someone with their garden. He'd usually warn her if he was going to be out when she woke, but then again, she'd slept in, and was running late for school. She showered, dried her hair then grabbed a granola bar before heading out to school.

Once there, she forgot her grandpa for a while, too busy staring at Riley's empty seat next to her. It was all so unreal. How had this all happened? Drew wanted more than anything to go back inside the hospital and search it, but she was too scared to go in alone. The cops had searched the place many times over, but even so, she still wanted to give it another try. At break time, she'd mentioned this to Ryan and Noah, who shook their heads and said, *No way*. Though she was angry, she understood their reasons. And yet she also felt a strong sense of duty to help her friend. She'd been unable to save her parents and now she had the tiniest chance of saving Riley. How could she ignore that? She made up her mind. She'd go inside before it got dark, so long as she could convince gramps to let her go out.

Never in a million years would he let her go back inside that hospital.

Her grandfather's car wasn't parked on the street when she got home, or the drive, and she wondered if it was at the repair shop. But that idea was soon put to rest as she unlocked the front door and walked inside. Like that morning, it was deadly silent. It didn't smell as if supper was cooking, either. She nearly always came home to Abe making one of his wonderful meals. The house had a cold feeling, which made goosebumps rise on her arms.

"Grampa, are you home?"

Not taking the time to kick off her shoes, she rushed to the kitchen, which looked exactly like it had this morning, before rushing to the stairs. What if he had collapsed upstairs and she'd left him all day? A sharp pain tore through her heart. She couldn't bear the thought of him lying there needing help, all alone.

At the top of her voice, she screamed, "Gramps!"

She was met by a heavy silence. At the top of the stairs, she stared at his bedroom door. Her knees trembled as she pushed it open. The room was empty. The bed was made, which meant he either hadn't slept in it or had made it before he left early this morning.

Drew couldn't shift the feeling that something was terribly wrong. She checked her own room, the bathroom and lastly the office. It was then her eyes landed on a cream envelope on the desk. Her name was written across it in her grampa's untidy scrawl. Drew swiped it off the jotter and ripped it open. For one, crazy moment she thought he'd written her a suicide note, that he'd missed his wife and son too much to carry on. Her eyes moist with unshed tears, she stared down at the note. The clock on the wall seemed to stop, like her heartbeat, as she read his words.

Dearest Drew,

I'm sorry. I can't stand by no more and watch this go on when I might be able to help. I'm going to the hospital to see if I can find Riley. I think I might be able to bring her back to you, and to Duane. I'm only sorry I wasn't brave enough to do this that first night you came home and told me what had happened. I want you to know that if I don't make it back, don't you dare show your face at that place. It's bad, it's evil and it's dangerous.

I've written you a list of instructions for what to do in the event of my death, my little cupcake. I hope it's not just yet but in case my time is up, then you need to know what you need to know. Go see Arnold Brown Solicitor in town. He has my actual will, and he will take care of you. He owes me big time so don't worry about a thing.

I love you more than anything, Drew. Take the money and get the hell out of Beacon as soon as you can, go start fresh in some place where the nightmares will eventually fade, and you can live a happy life.

Love always,

Gramps xxxx

The tears rolled down her cheeks freely now. He hadn't called her cupcake since she was a kid. A fluttering feeling inside her chest made it hard to breathe. Clutching the letter, she picked up the phone and rang Riley's house, hoping Duane would answer. It rang out. She tucked the letter into her back pocket and called the station where Dorothy answered.

As she explained about the letter, the words tripped out of her mouth so fast she already knew they wouldn't make sense.

"Honey, slow down, what's the matter with Abe? Do you need the paramedics?"

"He's not here. I can't find him. He's gone to the hospital to look for Riley and he hasn't come back."

"He didn't! Jeez, this is one big mess. Where are you? I'll get the chief to come see you when I can get hold of him. Right now, I can't find him either."

Drew caught her breath. She knew she had to get to the hospital. What else could she do? Besides it looked as if half the town were up there anyway. She didn't have a ride, so she messaged Ryan to pick her up ASAP. She saw the three dots on the screen then a thumbs up appeared. For a moment she wondered if she was being fair dragging him into this. Then she figured it was all partly his fault to begin with. If he hadn't suggested that they went inside that awful place, this nightmare wouldn't be happening.

TWENTY-THREE

The sky was getting darker by the second. Maria stared though the car window at the thunderclouds rolling in with a heavy feeling of dread. She loved a good storm and would purposefully try to get to the Empire State Building or the Top of the Rock to watch one rolling in over the city. If she wasn't a detective, she'd be a professional storm chaser. There was something about this one, though, that unsettled her. It also perfectly matched the mood she was in. What better occasion to travel back in time than during a thunderstorm?

Pulling up to the hospital entrance, they found the chief and Jimmy leaning against his pickup.

"I thought he had to get changed," Frankie muttered. "He's wearing the same clothes."

"He's got a different colored shirt on."

Frankie parked the car next to them and they all got out. Maria smiled at Jimmy. "This is Missy and Emilia, Jimmy."

Jimmy nodded at the two women. "Ladies, I think we need to get ourselves a plan together."

Missy raised her eyebrows. "I was hoping you already had one."

Jimmy indicated Maria. "She's the one with the wild plan. Now, does anyone have a better one because I already know the spirits are not happy. The great creator is sending a storm our way to stop us. He wants harmony and balance, not this."

Frankie stared at him. "I thought you had to get changed?"

"I did. This is my lucky shirt."

Frankie turned to Maria. "We're screwed."

The chief looked up at the sky. "Whatever we're doing, we need to take shelter because I don't like the look of those clouds. It's not safe to be out in this weather. We're going to be soaked through in seconds when the rain comes."

They all clambered into Duane's truck. The elderly women got in the front of the cab with the chief, while Frankie, Maria and Jimmy squeezed in the back.

It was Missy who spoke first. "That thing will know we're planning something, I bet. We need to cause a distraction so Maria can sneak in and get up to the tower on her own."

"What kind of distraction?" asked the chief.

"What if we started a contained fire?" suggested Missy. "It might think we're about to burn the place down."

Frankie's eyes almost rolled to the back of his head. "Hello, there's a storm on its way." As if to prove his point a brilliant flash of lightning zigzagged across the sky in the distance. "You really think you should be out here trying to light a fire?"

Duane sighed. "What do you suggest?"

Emilia spoke up. "What if we bless the perimeter of the building? That way we'll stop it escaping and make it feel trapped. That might encourage it to go back in time when Maria goes in there, and to take her with it."

Jimmy nodded. "I'll ask the great creator to help us to banish the evil one. If you ladies bless the outside at the same time, that should be a pretty good distraction."

Frankie glanced worriedly at Maria. "What about me and the chief? What are we supposed to do?"

Maria patted his arm. "You're going to wait by the entrance in case I need you. The chief is going to look after Missy and Emilia."

He let out his breath. "This is beyond stupid, Maria, and dangerous."

"But you'll do it because you always have my back. Don't come in unless you hear me call for you, Frankie. I mean it, promise me you won't?"

She knew she was being unfair to him. She was probably on the verge of giving him a coronary. And yet she felt as if she was being guided by some higher power, and, as scared as she was, she still knew she had to go on with her plan.

"You better holler loud if you want me. I'll be listening."

"Thank you."

Missy turned to Maria, uncapping a bottle of the holy water. She dipped her finger inside and made the sign of a cross on Maria's forehead. She passed a small vial of the water to her. "In case all else fails, throw this at it and tell it to be gone."

Maria took it from her, pushing it into her pocket. "If it's an ancient spirit, will it be bothered by holy water?"

Missy smiled at her. "I think it will still hold power over the spirit, but we'll have to see. Are you sure about this, dear? Would you rather I went in?"

"Absolutely not. That thing almost pushed me out of the window. I don't want you to get hurt." Maria could smell the woody, acrid smoke as Jimmy's fire took hold. She turned to see the orange flames licking against the rotting parts of the building that Frankie had stacked as kindling and she felt a small sense of satisfaction. When she was out of there, she was going to burn it to the ground. Fire was the best way to cleanse a building like this—possibly the *only* way.

She paused, not sure where that had come from. She normally didn't condone arson.

They gathered around the fire as another lightning strike

filled the now blackened sky in the distance and the thunder rumbled in the distance. It was so dark Maria thought if she looked out of the window, she'd think it was almost midnight, when it wasn't even six pm.

"It's time for me to go inside. I'll see you soon. Hopefully with Riley. If I don't come out, go looking for me in the retirement homes and come visit, okay?"

A pained expression came over Frankie's face. He didn't speak, as if he couldn't find the words.

The chief shook his head. "I should go. It's my daughter. I should be risking everything, not you."

Maria smiled at him. "This is my job, and I've faced this kind of evil before. That thing took a teenage girl and I think it will take a woman, too. It clearly prefers women to men. At least, there haven't been any reports of missing males who had been in here."

Before she could change her mind, she took the flashlight out of her pocket and walked toward the door. She didn't turn back to look at Frankie or Missy or Emilia, because she didn't want her faith and determination to waver. She prayed it wasn't her last chance to see their faces.

DECEMBER 1960

Abe opened his eyes, then blinked. He was on his back on a hard floor, that much he knew. He lifted a hand up so he could see his fingers and saw that they were as arthritic and wrinkled as they'd been ten minutes ago. Disappointment surged through him. So much for returning to his prime.

Pushing himself up onto his elbows, he sniffed the air. It smelled like a hospital tinged with the odor of something gone bad. He was still in the tower, but it wasn't falling to bits and the window was still intact. As he stood up, every bone in his body ached. He shook himself off and made his way to the window. His breath caught in the back of his throat. It looked just like it had when he'd worked it, all those years ago. The grounds were well kept, the topiary was trimmed, the lawns were cut, and patients were outside walking around with the nurses in the white uniforms and starched hats they used to wear that reminded him of paper boats. His surprise and nostalgia soon died away as he remembered what had brought him here. Where was that goddamn thing? Why was it hiding itself away?

He swiveled around. There was nothing there. He had to go

find Riley. He'd no idea yet how he'd get her back, but one step at a time. He went down the stairs to the tower door, only to find it was locked from the outside. *Of course,* he thought. At some point he'd put on a big bolt after the doc recommended that he do so. At the time it had been just another job on his never-ending to do list and he'd done it without questioning why. Now, he realized that the doc wasn't keeping people out of the tower; he was keeping something in, by bolting it from the outside.

Abe sat on the bottom step. *I'll be damned, they knew something was in here and they tried to keep it locked away all those years ago.* The thought made his skin crawl. Where was that thing now? Out on the prowl? That lock was never going to keep it out—or in. What were they thinking?

He rattled the door, hammered on the wood, cussing like a sailor.

"Hello, who's in there?"

He stopped. "I got locked in, can you let me out?"

There was a pause, and then a voice, so soft it felt like velvet kisses against his ears, said, "Hang on."

There was the sound of a bolt being drawn back, then the door opened. He found himself staring open mouthed at a petite, blonde-haired woman.

She smiled. "What happened? Have you been in there long?"

His head shook. "Only a few years."

Fear crossed her pretty blue eyes and he realized she probably thought he was a patient. "Sorry, bad joke. I do maintenance here and someone locked the door behind me." He saw the hospital band on her slender wrist and realized *she* was, in fact, a patient. "You look like a movie star, but I bet you get that all the time."

She threw back her head and laughed. "I do, as a matter of fact. My name is Faye, and you are?"

"Abraham, but everyone calls me Abe. Thank you, Faye, for rescuing me, I appreciate that."

She stared over his shoulder up the stairs with a fearful look in her eyes. "Say, you didn't see anything unusual up there, did you?"

He studied her. "No, why do you ask?"

She shrugged. "It's not often you see a lock on the outside, you know. It makes a person wonder why. I better get going, nice to meet you, Abe."

"Hey, you haven't seen a teenage girl, have you? Riley, she's got blonde hair, seventeen."

Faye stopped dead and turned around slowly. This time she looked him up and down. He wasn't dressed any differently to how he'd always dressed, ever since he was a teenage boy. Faded jeans, checked shirt, and boots. He must have dropped his thick winter coat.

"Why do you ask me that?" Her eyes narrowed. "Why do you want to know about a teenage girl?"

He debated whether to lie to her, but time was too short. "She's the best friend of my granddaughter, Drew, and she's missing. I've come to take her home."

Faye's eyes sparkled with tears. "Then you must be from the future, too?"

Startled, he nodded. The sound of voices came from the stairs, and the woman grabbed his arm and tugged him along the corridor to a door. Opening it, she shoved him inside, just as two nurses reached the top of the stairs. She ran in behind him and slammed the door shut. Seeing who was sat on the bed made his stomach drop to the floor.

"Abe!" Riley rushed toward him. He barely had time to open his arms before she crashed into him. She wrapped her arms around him, holding him tight. "What are you doing here? How did you find me?"

"I'm here to take you home, Riley."

Riley let out a sob. Faye gave a small whoop and clapped her hands with delight. "I'm not going to lie. I thought you were that *thing*, tricking me into letting you out."

"Then why did you open the door?"

She laughed. "Because I'm too nosy for my own good, and I didn't think a monster would ask quite so politely. Besides, that *thing* comes and goes as it pleases. It was here earlier."

Abe felt a stab of fear. "It was here? Then I don't suppose we have much time."

Voices outside the room made all three of them freeze. Faye stared at the door handle as it began to turn. She grabbed hold of Abe and pushed him toward the closet. He disappeared inside just as the nurse stepped into the room.

"I'm not sure what you two are up to, but I don't think the patients are supposed to be living in each other's rooms the way you are. This is a hospital, not a summer camp. Miss Miller, you best get back to your own room. The doctor wants to see you soon for a chat. Riley, you are coming down to group therapy, see if you can remember any more about how you got here."

The nurse's voice wasn't unkind, but it was authoritative. Neither of them wanted to give Abe's hiding place away. They would go to their sessions then meet back here when they were over.

Riley nodded and followed the nurse out into the hall. She turned back, and Faye winked at her mouthing, *I got this.*

TWENTY-FOUR

Maria didn't look back at Frankie. She knew he was silently pleading with her to do so, but she was scared that if she did, she wouldn't go through with this. Stepping inside that abandoned hospital was like entering another world. The air was charged with static electricity. Turning on the flashlight, she shone it in the direction of the staircase. The hairs on the back of her arm stood up. The stairs were lined with ghostly figures watching her every move. They looked as if they were made from wispy smoke, hovering off the ground, all eyes on her.

Taking a deep breath then releasing it, she said, "Hi, it's me again, Maria. I'm on my own this time. I'm not here to hurt you or be disrespectful, I'm here to save the girl. I also think I may be able to save you all, too, and set you free, if that's what you want. But first of all, I have to get to the tower and find a way to go back in time. Are you all cool with that?"

She didn't expect an answer, so was shaken to hear a yearnful collective whisper. She took a few steps into the semi-darkness, not sure if the ghosts would try to stop her. To her relief, they let her pass. As she walked by each one, the stray hairs of her ponytail stood on end, the way it did when someone rubbed a balloon across your hair. If she ever got to describe the ghosts to Frankie, she'd use the word 'mirage'. She felt as if she was in the desert passing an oasis.

The skin on the back of her neck suddenly became icy, as if strands of an invisible, frozen silk web were being spun around her. Still, she carried on. She found herself in the second-floor corridor, passing by rooms that had once held the rich and famous. Nothing bad had happened to her so far, so she felt emboldened. At least she hadn't had to battle the ghosts of a hundred dead patients before she got to the really terrifying part.

The door to the tower was wide open which made her pause; it was either expecting her, or someone had been here and not closed it. She wished she had a walkie-talkie on her just so she could hear Frankie's voice, but if she did, she'd likely turn around and run back out of here without keeping her promise to the lost souls who were waiting for her.

"Hello, is anyone up there?" Her voice echoed and she felt stupid. Was that how you addressed a centuries old evil spirit?

Her voice fell silent, and she shone the beam up the stairs. There was something at the top on the floor in a heap and her heart beat faster. She ran up, afraid it was a body. And yet she could deal with an actual body. She could run a "sudden death" case with her eyes closed. But when she was closer, she realized it was only a big, thick winter coat. Nudging it with the tip of her boot, she confirmed there was nothing solid inside. As she shone the flashlight downwards, she saw a faded name in permanent marker on the label. *Abe Dean.* She turned to see if he was nearby on the floor. The tower was empty, so why was Abe's coat here? She bent down to pick it up and got the faint scent of something awful. Maria dropped the coat as if it burned her fingers. A pulse in the side of her head began to throb. *Oh God, where is Abe?* Had he tried to find Riley? What had happened to him?

She opened her mouth and shouted at the top of her voice. "Abraham, where are you?"

Her voice echoed around the brick walls. A loud flash of lightning illuminated the small tower room and Maria let out a scream which was drowned out by an almighty crash of thunder. A black shadow in the corner was watching her. She realized it had been ever since she stepped inside the building. But it had waited until now to reveal itself.

Not sure whether she was insane to do so, Maria opened her arms and shouted: "Come get me, motherfucker!"

Then she ran forwards. Maria expected to hit the brick wall. Instead, she rushed into a jelly-like, squelching substance that consumed her whole. It was impossible to breathe with the stench of rotting flesh filling her mouth and nostrils, making her gag until she choked. She was aware of a huge bang, a flash of light, and then there was nothing, as the world she knew went black.

* * *

At the exact moment Maria ran into the soul collector, Frankie felt a pain shoot into his chest. Missy and Emilia both turned to him. "Are you okay?"

He shook his head, gasping as the pain eased. "It's taken her, it's taken Maria."

"It marked her from day one." Missy's voice was grave.

His fists clenched as he spoke through gritted teeth. "Why did you let her go inside there?"

"It was her choice. And she's still alive. I'm sure of it."

Frankie wanted to scream, to cry, to run into the hospital and find the son of a bitch himself and drag Maria to safety. But he didn't. He'd promised Maria that he'd look after the girls and that he'd only run inside if she called him.

Emilia nudged Missy. "We can't falter. We need to keep on."

They looked at him. "Can we continue?"

"Be my guest," he replied bitterly.

He turned away from them to see Jimmy moving around the fire. There was a shadowy figure beside him as if there were two Jimmys stepping in complete sync. Duane stood behind him, watching the fire and then the sky. The thunderstorm was almost upon them. There had been no rain yet, but the sky was rumbling, and the lightning was bright.

Frankie couldn't tear his gaze away from Jimmy. There were definitely two of him, a human and a shadow. His eyes closed, he repeated the same words over and over.

Twin lights came into view and Frankie wondered who was arriving at the hospital at this time. The car parked and its doors opened. He heard a girl's voice call out, "Duane, you've got to help me. I can't find my grampa. He's gone into the hospital."

The kid ran toward the chief and he held out his hands. "Drew, I need you to be real quiet now, and not disturb Jimmy, okay? How do you know Abraham is inside there?"

She sniffed loudly. "Because he left a note telling me... We have to go in and find him, Chief Holt. He thinks he can find Riley but how can he, how? She's not in there."

Duane placed his hands on Drew's shoulders. "Sweetheart, there is a cop inside there now. If Abe is in that hospital, she'll find him and bring him out. Trust me, we can't go in at the moment, not until Jimmy and the ladies have finished what they're doing."

"What are they doing?"

"Blessing this place—like it should have been blessed a long time ago. When it's time to go inside, I promise you I will find Abe and drag him out, but for now we just have to give them a little time to do their stuff. Can you go and wait in the car for me? Who's driving, Ryan?"

She nodded. "Go sit with him, Drew, and we'll go in together as soon as it's safe to do so."

She walked back toward the car and Emilia whispered, "Do you think he's really in there? He might have already found the girl and be on his way back with her. That would be good, wouldn't it?"

Frankie muttered, "It would be a miracle. But then what would happen to Maria?"

His question hung in the air. Nobody was brave enough to answer it.

TWENTY-FIVE

Maria finally managed to push her way out of its grasp. She landed with a crash against the brick wall and her shoulder crunched. Letting out a yelp of pain, she fell to the floor. She sat there for a moment, trying to gather the strength to move, as a wave of sickness rose through her. From her position on the floor, she gradually became aware that the tower was different. The window contained glass and bright daylight flooded through it. She'd no idea what time it was but the storm had vanished and it seemed like a pleasant day.

Pushing herself up with her good arm, she leaned against the wall and took deep breaths. She headed for the stairs and rushed down them. To her relief, the door was ajar. Stepping out into the hallway she took in the plush carpets and fresh paintwork. She could hear voices filtering up from the ground floor and so peeked over the banister. The great crystal chandelier that in Maria's own time was nothing but broken glass and rusted metal sparkled beautifully, casting tiny rainbows on the polished cherrywood floor beneath. A woman behind the reception desk was dressed in a smart suit and sipped from a mug.

There was a blood-curdling scream and Maria looked to see

a woman with limp, long, brown hair covering her face. She wore a white hospital gown and was being chased toward the desk by two burly orderlies. The woman slammed into the counter with such force that she must have winded herself, and the receptionist spilled the contents of her mug. The patient tried to clamber up to get to the receptionist, but the two orderlies took an arm each and dragged her away.

"What the hell, Burt? You have one job and that's to keep the patients under control, and you can't even manage that?"

Burt shrugged. "Sorry, Jeanie, she's quick. We didn't know she was going to make a run for it. Said she wanted the bathroom."

He winked at Jeanie and Maria felt sorry for the patient. She had come from one of the wards on the floor below her, or from the padded cells in the basement, and reminded Maria of the ghosts who'd tried to suck out her soul. Maria felt bad for her. She must have eventually died here—and for what purpose? A doorbell chimed and a moment later Maria heard male voices shouting and demanding to be let inside. With Jeanie kept busy, Maria took her chance to search for Riley and Abe, if he was here. She entered the first room she came to. Inside she found a woman in a smart two-piece suit, clutching a small suitcase. She stared at Maria in disbelief, and Maria realized she must look strange in her skinny jeans, boots and black shirt.

"Sorry, ma'am, wrong room."

She shut the door before the woman could ask her any questions. Trying room after room, she found they were all empty, including the last one, where the scent of Chanel No 5 lingered in the air, reminding her of Missy who never went anywhere without wearing it.

Next, she searched the floor below, where there were separate men's and women's wards. She turned into the women's ward and found a row of hooks with white clinicians' coats.

Taking one, she put it on with some difficulty, thanks to her broken shoulder. She picked up a clipboard left on a windowsill and strode along the corridor into the open ward. A nurse who'd been writing up notes behind a desk glanced up at Maria, then went back to her work. Maria scanned the beds. There were women asleep and sitting in chairs reading. Two older women were playing cards using a bed as a card table.

"Nurse, I'm looking for Riley Holt; is she under your care?"

The nurse looked up again for a second time. "Who?"

"Young girl, around seventeen. Riley Holt turned up here a few days ago."

"Oh, the mystery girl, she's called Riley Holt, huh? Poor kid didn't speak for forty-eight hours, she was so shocked. Dolores got her moved out of the dungeons up to the second floor, but I don't know what room she's in."

"Is Dolores around?"

The nurse shrugged. "Probably, but I couldn't tell you where she is. You're new here, doc, I haven't seen you before. Did they bring you in just for the kid?"

Maria nodded. "Yeah, they did. I'm still finding my way around."

"Oh, I see. They must be worried about her to do that. It's a bit of a maze but it won't take you long to get used to it. Have you tried upstairs in the guest rooms?"

"Yes, it's empty except for one patient waiting to go home."

The nurse lowered her voice. "Oh, she's not going home. Poor woman has been walking around with that little case since her husband dropped her off. He's a writer, apparently—he can't look after his wife and write at the same time, so he brought her here." She rolled her eyes as if to say, *men*, and Maria agreed with her. These were different times to her own. She tried to imagine being stuck here with such dated ways and realized it would be a nightmare trying to control herself and she'd probably end up sedated or given electric shock therapy.

"Thanks for your help, I'll go see if I can find her."

Maria exhaled as she walked away.

"Hey, doc?"

She paused. Did this woman know she was a fake?

"I'm Lucy, what's your name?"

"Maria."

"Good to meet you, Maria, welcome to the team. You should try the group therapy. They may have taken her to that, down on the ground floor."

"Thanks, Lucy, I'll do that."

The two women playing cards began to scream at each other and Lucy rushed toward them. Maria made her exit before she got asked to help because while she was great at arresting people and finding killers, she wasn't so good at being a caregiver. Feeling more confident with the clipboard tucked under her good arm, she walked down the hallway. There was a lot of noise coming from down below. Hurrying down the stairs she saw the group of angry men surrounding the reception desk where Jeanie was looking very flustered. One of the guys turned around and she stopped in her tracks. She knew him. Her pops and brother were huge baseball fans and cited this man as one of the best players of his time. His eyes locked with hers and she smiled. He didn't smile back; instead, his eyes were like twin swirling pools of anger.

"Hey, doc, do you know where my ex-wife is? This clown won't tell me. I'm here to take her home where she belongs. She doesn't belong here and I'm gonna kill that woman who put her in here."

Before Maria could answer, a nurse came rushing toward him. Maria recognized the much younger version of Dolores straight away. Dolores glanced at her and paused for a second, a look of confusion in her eyes. Then she shook her head and continued toward Joe.

"Sir, am I glad to see you; Miss Miller is in with the head

doctor, but I will go and get her now. Please be patient, you can see her very soon."

Dolores had a soothing, calming voice and the angry voices subsided as Joe motioned to the three men standing with him to quieten down.

As Dolores passed, Maria reached out for her arm gently and whispered, "Dolores, I'm looking for Riley."

The nurse stopped and stared at Maria. "I don't know you, do I?"

"Not at this time, but you will in the future."

She faltered, shaking her head, then seemed to make up her mind. "Okay, follow me, I'll show you where she is. Are you taking her home?"

"I hope so."

Dolores smiled. "Well, if today isn't full of surprises. What happened to your arm?"

Maria shook her head. "You don't want to know."

"Let me get Miss Miller. While I do that, you take Riley out of that group session and do whatever you have to do."

"Thank you."

Maria followed her along the hallway and Dolores pointed to a doorway on the right-hand side before carrying on to a room further along. Maria knocked on the door and stepped inside a room where six women and Riley sat in a semi-circle on wooden chairs.

A man in a white coat stared at Maria. "Yes?"

"Sorry to disturb you, doctor, but I'm here to take Riley out."

He stared at Maria, looking her up and down. "Who said you could interrupt my session?" Before she could answer, the door burst open, and the big orderly rushed into the room.

"Christ, Burt, what the hell is going on?"

"Doc, you're going to want to see this. Guess who is at the front desk?"

"I don't care if Jesus Christ has put in an appearance, Burt, we're in session."

"But it's the baseball player, he's here to collect her."

The doctor stood up. "Ladies, excuse me whilst I deal with Burt. I'll be back soon, and I'll discuss this matter with you when I come back, Doctor—?"

"Doctor Miller."

He gave a curt nod then followed an excited Burt out of the room. Maria didn't waste any time.

"Riley, I'm here to take you back. You need to come with me, sweetie."

Riley jumped out of her chair and rushed toward her. They hurried out of the room and down the corridor where they heard the commotion in reception. That's when they saw her.

Like she had walked right off a film set, the Hollywood actress Maria had long admired sashayed straight over to them. She stopped in front of Riley, pulled her into a warm embrace then whispered, "Remember what I said. If you don't like it, come back and find me. I won't ever forget you, Riley. Thank you for making me smile and giving me hope."

Riley hugged her back fiercely. "I will. Please take care of yourself and forget about the others."

The woman gave Riley a huge smile and winked at her, then she turned to Maria. "Look after her, she's special."

And then she ran toward the desk, calling out, "Joe!"

Maria grabbed Riley's arm and tugged her toward the stairs. "We have to get to the tower; we don't have much time."

They were halfway up the stairs when Riley stopped. "Wait! We have to get Abe. He's waiting for me in my room."

Maria felt a warm rush of love toward the old guy who'd risked everything to come rescue his granddaughter's friend. "Go get him, quick."

Riley ran to her room. When she reappeared with Abe a moment later, his mouth fell open. "Well, I'll be damned."

She grinned. "Looks like we had the same idea. Come on, we haven't got long." They rushed toward the tower door and when they reached it, Maria paused, turning back to them both.

"I don't know how this is going to work or even if it will, but there are people blessing the hospital in our time to stop the soul collector from escaping, to trap it. We need to force it to take us back to our own time."

They filed through the tower door and Maria closed the door behind them. It was darker than when she'd arrived and it was much cooler, too.

It was waiting for them up the stairs, Maria knew that. But they had no choice other than to face it. Doing so was their only way to return home.

TWENTY-SIX

The trio were almost at the door to the attic when a dark figure stepped out of the shadows. Its head was bent forwards, long strands of greasy hair covering its face. It might have seemed like a patient from downstairs who had found their way up to the guest rooms, but Maria knew this was no lost patient. That thing in the tower was using this corrupted soul to do his work, letting it pass through space and time. He slowly lifted his head, and a long line of drool hung from his parted lips that curled back into a monstrous grin.

Abe stepped forward. "We have no business with you, fella. We just need to get up to the tower if you'd kindly let us pass."

The ghost or ghoul—Maria wasn't sure which—slowly tilted its head to one side as its grin stretched so wide the skin cracked and tore, dots of blood forming where it had split. Maria grabbed hold of Abe's arm, tugging him back, and then moved in front of him and Riley.

"I know you. I know that you're Malcolm Collins and I don't think you want to be here, Malcolm. I think this spirit has been controlling you. It's going to make you do terrible things for a long time, during your lifetime and even afterwards. I need you to step to one side and let us pass, please."

It opened its mouth and began to laugh, only the sound was more like a high-pitched buzzing noise, the kind a swarm of bees makes, and Maria knew what was going to happen as a cloud of bees exploded from its mouth.

"Duck!" she screamed and all three of them fell to the floor. The bees swarmed around them and Maria pulled out the bottle of holy water, uncapped it and threw some up toward the insects. The deafening noise stopped as the bees disappeared into thin air. She heard Riley sob as she stood up straight and stepped closer to him.

"I don't believe you were fully in control of yourself when you murdered those kids. I don't think you could have stopped what happened even if you tried. You came to this place for refuge and found something so evil that it took over your heart and soul, turning you into nothing more than its pawn."

Maria remembered all she'd read about him in her research. Malcolm Collins had once been a regular guy who'd been down on his luck after his wife threw him out and he lost his job. He'd come to the hospital looking for somewhere dry to stay for a couple of nights, while he tried to find work. He'd walked into this place, sad, drunk and a little angry at what his life had become, but he hadn't been a violent man. Maria had read the news articles where his ex-wife Vera cried saying she didn't know how he had done such awful things. He wasn't the man she'd known. And now Maria knew she was right. He'd been taken over. The ghostly shadow of Malcolm Collins looked up at Maria and fixed its gaze on her. A flicker of what looked like pain passed over its eyes. Even though he'd done terrible things, she felt sorry for the guy inside the monster.

"You can stop this now, Malcolm. You can stop doing what the soul collector tells you to do and let us pass. When we get to the other side, we will set you free, I promise you that. I have no idea about heaven or hell, but I think you have served your time in hell whilst you've been a captive here. Wouldn't you like your soul to be free? Wouldn't you like to see Vera again?"

A light shone inside the twin, black holes that had been his eyes at the mention of Vera's name. "Vera never believed you were a monster, so why don't you prove to her that you aren't?"

There was a roar so loud that Malcolm clamped his hands to his ears. She'd made the soul collector angry. That must be a sign her plan was working. Malcolm tilted his head, turned and stumbled toward the railing, gripping it tight. Then he glanced back at Maria, before launching himself over the edge, leaving the access to the tower door clear.

TWENTY-SEVEN

Missy and Emilia had almost completed the circle of the building. The only part left was the entrance which they would bless as soon as Maria and Riley came out of the building. Frankie hoped that Maria was already on her way back, having found both Riley and Abe. Not for the first time, he wished he hadn't dragged Maria into this. He was to blame if she didn't come out of that hospital. He would never live with the guilt, and he'd never stop searching for her.

He tried to imagine what it would be like to see Maria in her eighties, maybe even her nineties; he wasn't good at math. Maria with grey hair and crow's feet. He felt sure she'd have plenty of laughter lines because she was a good woman with a great sense of humor. He would love every single one of those well-earned lines on her face because it would have meant that she'd survived whatever horror was inside that hospital, even if he'd lost her. He'd still have memories of the times they'd shared together, which were too precious to ever forget.

Hot tears stung the back of his eyes. Would she live a happy life, get married, have children and be surrounded by grand-kids? God, he hoped so. No one deserved happiness more than

Maria. She would make a great mom and grandma. She kept all that love buried inside her—she'd probably smother them all with the intensity of it. Tears fell down his face. He was no longer able to contain them.

"Frankie?" said Missy.

He swiped his cheek and turned to her. "What?"

She pointed to the tower. "Something is happening?"

He stared up at the window. It had a pane of glass. Then the glass was gone, and it was back to being a black hole. It kept changing, though, from glazed to open.

"What's going on?"

Huge drops of rain began to fall around them. It gathered in intensity until it was torrential, and the sound of the water hammering against the hospital was deafening. Thunder and lightning cracked above their heads, and Frankie ushered the two elderly women under the porch for protection. A bolt of lightning hit a tree not too far away from where he and Duane stood. The rain was putting out the fire Jimmy had started. Drew and Ryan left the car and ran toward the porch where Frankie, Missy and Emilia huddled. Duane grabbed Jimmy by the arm and dragged him to join them. Drew was crying and shaking.

"What's happening? I wish we'd never come to this stupid place."

Frankie looked at the kid. He wanted to say, *Me, too.* Instead, he glanced up at the tower, which was still flitting between the present and the past. Jimmy looked up as well, his expression grim.

"We have to wait. What happens next is in the hands of the great creator and your friend. We have done all that we can. It's down to a battle that has been ongoing since time began—the battle of good against evil."

The sodden group huddled together, all watching the tower that loomed over them with wide eyes and open mouths.

* * *

All three reached the top of the steps. Riley whimpered as her eyes fell across it, standing there waiting for them. Up until then, it had been nothing but smoke and dark shadows. Seeing its true form, Maria instinctively crossed herself. It was over seven feet tall and filled the space in front of the window. But it was its eyes that terrified Maria the most. She'd seen them before and had almost been consumed by those two white discs. Its snout, bearing the longest, sharpest teeth she'd ever seen, dripped with saliva. As they stared at it, it watched them.

Maria tried to think about what Missy had told her. Her belief in light and good would help her survive. She reached into her pocket for the small bottle of holy water Missy had given her. It was so small compared to the size of the monster, but it also felt warm and powerful. Behind the snarling thing the air was hazy as if it was a hot summer day, and Maria knew then it was trying to stop them from getting to it. She was certain that glitch in the air was what had brought them to the past and was their means of escape. Somehow it had separated from the beast, as he'd grown weaker. Abe, stood between them, reached down and took hold of Riley's hand on one side and Maria's on the other. They stood there, all three of them scared, but defiant, ready to do battle with the terrifying beast before them.

Abe kissed the top of Riley's head, whispering in her ear, "Take care of Drew and live a happy life, kid."

Maria felt a lump in her throat. She knew what he was going to do. "We can do it together, there's no need, Abe."

He shook his head. The monster mirrored him, its eyes fixed on him. It had picked him out as the biggest threat. Abe took a step toward it; it did the same.

"Don't fool with me, old man. I will snap you in two." Its voice was raspy, as if it hadn't used it for a very long time.

Abe laughed. "That would be something, I'd like to see you try."

It moved toward Abe. The floorboards shook with the weight of it. Maria reached out for Riley's hand and took tight hold of it.

"What did you think? That I'm going to let all three of you go?"

"I'll tell you what is going to happen," Abe replied. "You're scared because somehow you lost your grip on whatever you've been doing here. Maybe it's because you've run out of souls to feed off, I don't know. But it happened with that girl the College Kid Killer brought here, and you thought it was a one off. Now it's happened again, and again, and again. You've lost control. Instead of being devoured by you, we've found ourselves here. I can tell you're scared of us, and you know why? Because we didn't let you take our souls." Maria saw its long, bear-like claws swipe through the air toward Abe. It caught his side, tearing his flesh open so that his shirt bloomed with a flower of red. Abe never faltered. He kept on until he was grappling with it, his arms grasping the hideous creature.

"Go, now!" Abe screamed.

There was nothing Maria could do to help him. But there was a gap big enough for her and Riley to reach the space behind the creature. She dragged a screaming Riley by the hand to the window behind the creature. As she did, she tossed the rest of the bottle of holy water to Abe who caught it with one hand. Maria and Riley launched themselves at the light and were sucked forwards with a loud whooshing sound. The last thing Maria heard was a guttural scream that she knew was the monster, and then she hit the floor with a loud thud.

Stunned, and in complete darkness, they lay on the cold wet floor of the tower. Rain poured through the open hole of the window. Maria crawled to her feet. She didn't know how much time they had, or how long Abe could stall the creature before it followed them. She tugged at Riley, who was glassy eyed, and dragged her down the stairs and out onto the second-floor hallway when the ground above them shook as something heavy hit the wooden floorboards. She knew without a doubt it was coming for them.

"Run!" Maria screamed to Riley, who had come to a stop, her whole body shaking with fear. Maria knew if they didn't get out of here now, it was over. It would kill them this time. Once again grabbing Riley's hand, she ran to the stairs. That's when she saw them—hundreds of figures lining the stairs and the hallway. Had they come to stop them from escaping?

A soft voice whispered in her ear, "Go, we will stop it. Thank you."

Tears filled Maria's eyes, blurring her vision. Together, Maria and Riley passed by the trapped souls, who closed the gap behind them. Despite the pain in her shoulder, Maria picked up the pace and they both ran for their lives. They pounded down the stairs, until they reached the ground floor and the front door. They didn't look back, even when she heard an unearthly scream fill the entire hospital, and then they were through the door, falling through it onto the porch.

"Riley!" Duane screamed his daughter's name.

"Frankie!" Maria screamed. "Seal the goddamn door."

Frankie slammed the door shut behind them and turned the key. Missy was behind him. She and Emilia as well as Jimmy finished their blessing of the building. Emilia took out a bag of salt for good measure and spread a line of it in front of the door.

"Where's my grampa?" Drew whimpered as there was an almighty crash from the tower above, and a figure came hurtling out of the open window, arms wide. Hitting the broken, rotting roof, it fell straight through and landed with a sickening thud on the floor.

TWENTY-EIGHT

Maria felt her heart break. Drew screamed and ran to him. She cradled his broken body on the floor. "Gramps, oh my God. Please don't die, I love you."

Abe's eyes fluttered open, and he smiled at his granddaughter, the light of his life, and whispered, "Did I tell you who I met? She called herself Faye. She was so beautiful, the image of Marilyn." He began to cough up blood, his breathing slowing as he took his last breaths. He whispered, "I love you, Drew."

As Drew cried over the broken, bleeding body of Abe, Duane hugged Riley closer and whispered, "Thank you, Abe." Missy knelt, taking the last few drops of holy water from the bottle he was clutching and shaking them onto his forehead to make the sign of the cross. Jimmy shook his head and looked around. Maria followed his gaze up to the tower. "What's wrong?"

"Oh man, it's contained for now, but we need to do more."

Maria looked at the tree burning from the lightning strike. It was now or never. She sprinted across to the tree, and grabbed a smoking log off the fire, Frankie and Jimmy following her lead. Duane looked on in horror realizing what they were going to do, then he shrugged, ran for a branch of his own and waited for it to set alight. The four of them stood by the front door, flames taking hold of the branches and logs they were clasping.

Duane nodded, opened the door and they threw them inside, closing the door quickly before they could go out. Then they stepped back and waited for the flames to take hold. It didn't take long before an orange glow could be seen behind one of the filthy panes of glass in the door.

Duane and Frankie carried Abe's body to safety away from the building. Duane covered Abe with a foil blanket he'd taken from the cab of his truck, and Drew knelt beside him, holding his hand, crying. The rest of them stood around, paying their respects to a man they'd barely known but who had given his life to save a teenage girl. Emilia shook Missy's arm and whispered, "Look up there."

All of them looked up to where the tower was now well ablaze. There was a pure white light shining in the sky so bright that they had to cup their hands over their eyes. It shone down onto the tower, and they watched as one by one, hundreds of ghostly figures were drawn up toward it, floating high into the sky.

"We set all those poor souls free," Missy cried.

Maria, who didn't cry in public, began to sob and Frankie wrapped his arm around her. Jimmy nodded in amazement. "Guess my lucky shirt worked, huh?"

Duane laughed. "I guess it did, Jimmy. I don't know how to thank you all for what you've done. You saved my girl and saved all of those, what are they?"

Missy answered, "Trapped souls who are now free to finally be reunited with their loved ones."

Drew's voice was broken. "What about grampa?"

Missy took hold of her hand. "Oh honey, your grampa is with your dad and your grandma. He's telling them all about the time he met a Hollywood actress. His body is a broken shell, my darling, but his spirit is not. He is the brightest light up there and you have to carry on for him. He wouldn't want you to give up. Look at what he's helped to do. So much love and light in a place that has known nothing but darkness and fear."

"Why didn't he tell us that she was a patient at the hospital? He used to watch all of her movies over and over."

Riley smiled. "It wasn't his story to tell, but he did meet her, and she was amazing."

Frankie turned to Maria. "Did you meet her?"

She shook her head. "I met a beautiful woman called Faye Miller; she's Riley's friend, isn't she, Riley?"

Riley nodded. "I'll never forget her, or Abe, or you. Thank you. I don't even know what you're called."

"I'm Maria Miller."

Riley gasped. "Are you any relation?"

"Not that I know of, but it would have been a pretty cool connection, eh?"

Frankie shrugged. "I have no idea what you guys are talking about, but I think we need to get your shoulder looked at, Maria. It doesn't look so good to me, and can I just say how much I really like that streak of white at the front of your bangs? It's giving me all the Lily Munster vibes."

A pain shot up her arm at the mention of her broken shoulder and she grimaced. Touching her bangs with her good arm, she said, "I've gone white?" He nodded and she laughed. "I'll take a few white hairs over the alternative. I'll survive, but now that you mention it, some Advil wouldn't go amiss."

Duane's phone rang, and he answered it. There were a lot of okays, uh-huhs and yeahs before he ended the call and turned to them.

"That was the professor—she managed to get DNA from the unknown bones and fast tracked it. They came back as a match for Courtney Moon, which is good news for her family, I suppose, after all this time. They can finally get the closure they need. I asked about the second body, and she seemed confused. Said there was only one set of remains recovered from the grave."

Maria smiled at him and pointed to Riley. "Don't ask me how or why, but it seems to me like we saved Riley while she still had a need for her bones. Why we remember and she doesn't, well, we'll have to chalk that one up to the wonders of the universe and be thankful for small mercies."

Sirens in the distance sounded as the last light in the sky began to dim. The hospital was ablaze and for one time only, Maria was glad to have committed a serious crime. That place needed razing to the ground, for new life to begin again. She hoped Beacon would finally be rid of the evil that had tainted it for so many years, and the living would come back to this land that had spent far too long harboring the dead.

A LETTER FROM THE AUTHOR

I'd like to say a huge thank you for reading *Her Lost Soul*. I hope you were hooked on Maria Miller's journey. If you want to join other readers in hearing about my new releases and bonus content, you can sign up for my newsletter:

www.stormpublishing.co/helen-phifer

If you enjoyed this book and could spare a few moments to leave a review, that would be amazing and hugely appreciated. Even if you're like me and only write short reviews they can make all the difference to encourage other readers to discover my books for the first time. Thank you so much!

I love reading scary stories that make the hairs on the back of my neck stand on end and hope this one gives you the cold chill that a good spooky tale should invoke. I first got the idea for kick-ass homicide detective Maria Miller when I went on a walking ghost tour of Greenwich Village in New York. It was a late summer's evening, as the sun began to set, and the sky started to turn that velvety black I love so much against the backdrop of the stunning New York skyline. As the tour guide walked us through Washington Square Park and through the streets, pointing out the buildings steeped in so much history, I knew I had to write about this area.

I wanted to write a thriller with a paranormal element to it —after all, there are so many ghostly tales about the city's buildings and the encounters residents have had. I knew that it would be interesting to combine the two with a tough native New York city cop. I thought that it would be a stand-alone story, but as I neared the end of *The Haunting on West 10th Street*, I knew I couldn't leave Maria and Frankie there. I loved the characters so much; at some point I would have to write more about them. Thanks to Storm, that yearning to continue their stories has been possible and I couldn't be happier that you are now a part of this wild ride through the streets of New York with Frankie and Maria.

Thanks again for being part of this amazing adventure with me and I hope you'll stay in touch—I have so many more stories to entertain you with!

Love Helen xx

facebook.com/Helenphifer1
x.com/helenphifer1
instagram.com/helenphifer
tiktok.com/@helen.phifer

ACKNOWLEDGMENTS

Where to start? The biggest thank you goes to my wonderful editor and all-round lovely person Kate Smith. I'm so sorry, Kate, this one was hard work but thanks to you it all makes sense now. I'll try to go easy on you with the next one!

A massive thanks to my copyeditor Natasha Hodgson for all her hard work, too. A big thank you goes to the lovely Alexandra Holmes for her amazing input. It's very much appreciated. I always say it takes a whole team to turn the rough draft of the story I write into the book you are reading or listening to and for that I'm eternally grateful to the rest of the fabulous Storm team for every part you play.

A huge thank you to the wonderful Oliver Rhodes for giving me the chance to bring these stories to life—it's so great to be working with you again.

Thank you to you, the beautiful person who has read this book and is still reading the acknowledgments. It's thanks to your amazing support that I'm able to live out my dream life of writing stories and sharing them with you. Every book bought, page read, audiobook listened to makes my heart so happy. That I get to share my sometimes crazy ideas with the world is just flabbergasting and I love it when you get in touch with me to tell me what you loved—and occasionally what you didn't love. Keep on being the most amazing human that you are; the world is a better place with you in it.

A huge thank you to Gina, Amanda, Yanira, Afy and Jassiel for reading all of my books from the very beginning for your book club. That is some dedication, and I can't thank you enough.

Thank you also to Paul O'Neill who will by the time you're reading this have been brave enough to give my story its final read through. I honestly couldn't do this without you, Paul.

As always, a heartfelt thank you to my family: Steve, Jess, Josh, Jerusha, Jaimea, Jeorgia, Danielle, Tom, Deji, Gracie, Donnovan, Laurence, Matilda, Bonnie, Sonny and Sienna. I love you all more than you could ever know and I'm so proud of you all for being so wonderful.

Until next time, take care. I love you all xx

Printed in Great Britain
by Amazon

40123513R00138